FREYJA

This edition first published in 2025 by Red Wheel,
an imprint of Red Wheel/Weiser, LLC
With offices at:

65 Parker Street,
Suite 7
Newburyport
MA 01950
www.redwheelweiser.com

Text copyright © 2025 L. Dean Lee
Illustrations copyright © 2025 Matt Greenway

All rights reserved. No part of this publication may be
reproduced or transmitted in any form or by any means,
electronic or mechanical, including photocopying,
recording, or by any information storage and retrieval
system, nor used in any manner for purposes of training
artificial intelligence (AI) technologies to generate text
or imagery, including technologies that are capable of
generating works in the same style or genre, without
permission in writing from Red Wheel/Weiser, LLC.
Reviewers may quote brief passages.

ISBN: 978-1-59003-578-8
EISBN: 978-1-63341-385-6

Conceived, edited, and designed by
Quarto Publishing, an imprint of
The Quarto Group
1 Triptych Place
London SE1 9SH
www.quarto.com

QUAR: 904527

Commissioning editor: Lily De Gatacre
Editor: Charlene Fernandes
Copy-editor: Caroline West
Assistant editor: Elinor Ward
Design: Karin Skånberg
Cover and original design: Martina Calvio
Illustrator: The Saxon Storyteller
Production manager: David Hearn
Art director: Martina Calvio
Managing editor: Emma Harverson
Publisher: Lorraine Dickey

Printed in China

10 9 8 7 6 5 4 3 2 1

FREYJA

AN ILLUSTRATED GUIDE TO THE GODDESS OF MAGIC, LOVE, AND WAR

BY L. DEAN LEE

Red Wheel

CONTENTS

Preface — 6

CHAPTER 1: BRIDGING THE CULTURAL GAP

Introduction — 10
The purpose of folklore and mythology — 12
How do we define a "god"? — 14
The Norse cosmos — 16
Vanaheim — 19
The Norse entities — 20

CHAPTER 2: WHO IS FREYJA?

Freyja's name — 26
Freyja's personality — 27
Freyja's appearance — 30
Freyja's characteristics — 32
Freyja's associations — 33
Notable possessions — 37
Freyja and flowers — 38
Freyja and cats — 40
Freyja and the disir — 42
Freyja's family and important relations — 44
Freyja and Frigg — 51
Freyja and jewelry — 52
Freyja and Gullveig — 54

CHAPTER 3: FREYJA IN MYTHOLOGY AND FOLKLORE

A note for the reader — 58
The Aesir-Vanir war — 60
Freyja escapes marriage — 62
The forging of Brisingamen — 67
The theft of Freyja's necklace — 68
Freyja's life in Asgard — 70

The theft of Thor's hammer	72
Freyja rides with Hyndla	76

CHAPTER 4: FREYJA IN THE WORLD

Freyja before and during the Viking Age	82
Freyja in medieval times	84
Freyja's early modern-day representations	89
Freyja today	90

CHAPTER 5: VENERATING FREYJA

How to venerate Freyja	94
Building an altar	95
Blót, or offerings	96
How to make an offering	97
Freyja's favorite offerings	100
Seid and practicing seid	103
Freyja's special days	110
Communicating with Freyja	111
Methods of communication	112
A courage ritual with Freyja	114
The tools of discernment	116
Closing notes on Heathenry	119

Glossary	120
Index	126
Acknowledgments	128

PREFACE

Despite being a Heathen for going on ten years now, I've only very recently sat down with Freyja. And I must say, I'm rather annoyed with myself that I put it off for so long. Freyja's not a deity I ever thought I'd work with, seeing as she very much represents something that I've failed to comprehend in the past—femininity and womanhood.

However, upon meeting Freyja for the first time, I realized that I was just getting bogged down in my own thoughts, and that my confusion came from the fact that I was conflating the *romanticized idea* of femininity with the *actual, realized expression* of femininity. These are, in fact, two different things. And it turns out that the latter is not at all unfamiliar.

I've felt Freyja's energy before in Wonder Woman, in the role of Barbie, in Astrid from the movie *How to Train Your Dragon*, and in people I've encountered in my life and in students I've taught. Freyja's the spirit of every little girl I've ever met who hated following the rules and instead wanted to build empires out of sticks and rocks. But she's also every

teen and young adult who wishes to live large and experience all that the world has to offer.

Who Freyja is as a person is everything that every young girl has ever envisioned herself to be: A celebrated hero, a powerful sorceress, and a respected warrior, one who's as beautiful as she is strong and capable.

All of these attributes are the goddess Freyja.

What's so fascinating is that Freyja basically operates as the younger complement to another goddess of the Norse pantheon—Frigg, who represents the married woman. Here, we seem to have two phases of womanhood represented by two figures, with Freyja being the younger variation with lots of energy, and Frigg the older and wiser one who has learned much from the experiences life has offered her.

In many ways, learning all this about Freyja has made her book much easier to write; she represents the lived experiences of girls and women alike. But in other ways it has added a greater layer of complexity. Freyja doesn't conform to our modern idea of "femininity," meaning she can't be quantified using the flat, idealized picture of womanhood to which we may default. She's literally every variation of it that exists, including everything we'd consider "un-lady-like." But as "the lady" herself, she gets to decide what that means.

This book explores all there is to know about Freyja, including what role she might have played in the Norse worldview. It has been a great privilege to work with her in its creation, and it's my hope that you find it a joy to read.

Skål!

L. DEAN LEE

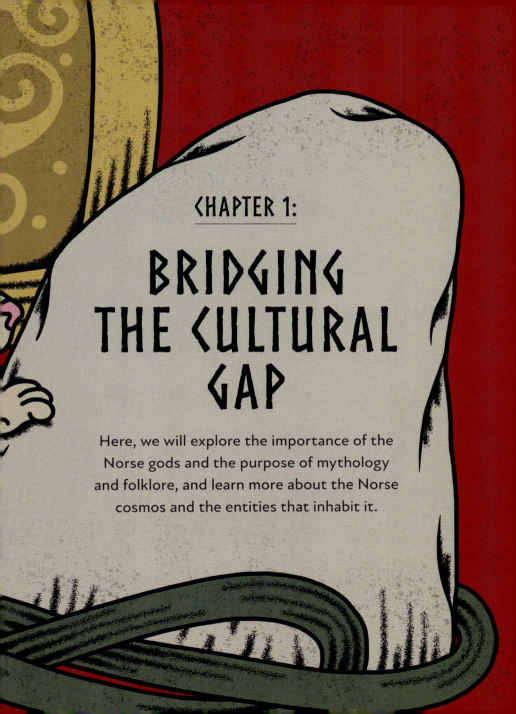

CHAPTER 1:
BRIDGING THE CULTURAL GAP

Here, we will explore the importance of the Norse gods and the purpose of mythology and folklore, and learn more about the Norse cosmos and the entities that inhabit it.

INTRODUCTION

Freyja is not an insignificant goddess by any means within the Norse pantheon. Even those with only a surface-level familiarity with the Norse gods might recognize her as the goddess of love, beauty, war, and magic. This is very true, and very much embodies her popular depiction.

The Norse people originated as a pre-Christian culture that lived in what we now call the Nordic countries—Norway, Sweden, Denmark, Iceland, Finland, Åland Islands, Greenland, and the Faroe Islands. Most of these countries are located in the northern European region known as Scandinavia.

The Norse are famous for venturing out into the world as Vikings during the Viking Age (793–1066 CE) in bygone times. However, "Viking" was a rather niche occupation, and most of the Norse people lived out rather typical lives as farmers, craftsmen, fishermen, parents, petty highwaymen, and more.

The pagan cultures of Scandinavia began to shift with the introduction of Christianity around the beginning of the Viking Age. Through a process of converting Scandinavian kings, the "old ways" fell out of popularity in favor of the "new ways" of Christianity. By the end of the Viking Age, the region had become fully Christian.

However, much of the Viking culture and folklore endured, and can still be found today among modern-day Scandinavians. The Norse myths and gods remain an important staple of culture throughout the Nordic countries for this reason.

WHO IS FREYJA?

Freyja's role is as the goddess of love, beauty, war, and magic. What isn't embodied within the popular depiction of Freyja is how these concepts are regarded within the Norse view of the world. If we are guided by the typical way we think of love, beauty, war, and magic, we may be tempted to interpret Freyja as a cross between the Greek goddesses Aphrodite and Athena.

But this isn't the case. Unlike the way we view the Greek gods, Freyja doesn't represent virtues, values, or ideals. Instead, she represents a memory.

Think back to when you were a little girl… or if you're not female, think back to the little girls you saw playing make-

believe when you were growing up. Remember the dolls, their accessories, and their playsets. Do you also remember how thematically designed they were, with all their pinks and purples and genre-specificity?

Now, if you've ever spent time being a girl or playing with girls, you'll know that their creativity is not limited by the design of the toy they are playing with. Even Barbie, with her endless careers, can barely hold a candle to the genre-defying capabilities of the typical five-year-old's imagination. At some point, said five-year-old will pull Barbie and her pink convertible car into an epic space adventure or take her downtown to adopt a dragon.

In this world of endless potential, a girl designs herself however she likes. She's a princess, a superhero, and a warrior all at once. She's capable of whatever she wants in that moment: She sees the future, has formidable magical powers, possesses fantastical familiars, and is fearless whenever battle or conflict arrive on her doorstep.

Remember in your body what this environment feels like, and what it was like to do whatever you imagined. This is Freyja's energy, and the sensation of endless capability is her "hall."

The Norse people evidently didn't believe that girls were supposed to outgrow this energy, as everything about Freyja encourages them to take it into adulthood. She wouldn't be a goddess otherwise.

Before we talk in more detail about Freyja, we first need to discuss the role mythology plays within Norse society.

THE PURPOSE OF FOLKLORE AND MYTHOLOGY

In order to comprehend Freyja, we need to understand the purpose of Norse mythology and Scandinavian folklore. Knowing what function the stories serve will lead to a better understanding of Freyja's role within them.

The Norwegian writer Jan Sigurd Horn describes mythology as "[humanity's] way of expressing the knowledge we have about the metaphysical reality we believe in." We often think of mythology as a collection of static and unchanging spiritual stories, or as a history of the gods. But this impression likely comes from the fact that we often learn about mythologies through written records, which are in and of themselves static and unchanging. A living mythology is far more dynamic. Simply put, a society's mythology is the narratives it tells itself about who it is and how life works.

IS MYTHOLOGY A DIVINE HISTORY?

We may be tempted to view Norse mythology as a history of all the things the gods have done. But the Norse myths are not a history, nor can they really represent one, since they don't actually have a chronological order; they're only put into some kind of order when compiled for a written anthology. Additionally, some stories have multiple regional variations, while other stories may be local to one particular community.

THE FUNCTION OF MYTHOLOGY

Mythology is a way for a culture to form an identity, an understanding of itself, and a paradigm of how it fits into the fabric of all things. It also provides a vehicle for education and a way to describe the forces and phenomena of the universe. But perhaps most of all, it's a vector through which we make sense of the world we live in and our relationship to it.

The mythology of the Norse people grew organically out of the culture itself, rather than being something that was taught to them by a religious leader or scripture. The myths were allegories that were used to explain real events, encapsulating through the medium of stories what it felt like to live on Earth.

These allegories were important because, by explaining abstract phenomena in terms of a felt-experience, the Norse people could make the world seem like a less unknowable place to live. So when they saw the edges of the world at the peaks of mountains and in the depths of volcanoes, they were already familiar with the character of these things due to the stories they had been told of hostile giants who embodied these wild landscapes. It may have been the stories making the world a familiar place that gave the Vikings their famed courage to explore the world.

SOURCES OF NORSE MYTHOLOGY

We can often get a sense of a culture's entire mythology by looking at different records of it from various times and

places, and seeing how it's changed. Unfortunately, Norse mythology offers very few things to guide us. Despite the fact that the Norse people had a writing system, the mythological texts that we do have mostly date from after the conversion to Christianity.

That isn't to say their mythology can't be trusted at all, however. We're lucky to have a few very important snapshots of Norse mythology that we can reasonably assume are authentic.

The Poetic Edda

The *Poetic Edda* is a collection of anonymous Old Norse poems, many of them pertaining to the gods. There are several versions in existence, many of which can be found in the *Codex Regius*, an Old Icelandic manuscript thought to have been written around 1270 CE. Although the *Codex Regius* (which means "Royal Book" or "King's Book") was written nearly 200 years after Scandinavia's Christianization, the stories it contains are much, much older and represent the pre-Christian mythology of the Norse people.

The Prose Edda

The *Prose Edda* is a mythography written by Icelandic lawspeaker and politician Snorri Sturluson in around 1220 CE. The book is composed of three parts: *Gylfaginning* ("The Tricking of Gylfi"), *Skáldskaparmál* ("The Language of Poetry"), and *Háttatal* ("Tally of Meters"). The first two books, *Gylfaginning* and *Skáldskaparmál*, recall a series of myths and legends about the Norse gods.

Despite the fact that Snorri was a Christian politician writing for a Christian audience during a time when paganism was heavily frowned upon, he actually did a great deal to preserve the Norse myths in their original form, wrapping them in a very thin disclaimer of "these aren't really gods, but nobles from Troy!" before launching into the Norse tales as they would have likely been remembered.

The purpose of Snorri's book was essentially a political one. Snorri was very keen for Iceland to unite under King Hakon the Fourth of Norway, and so he wrote the *Prose Edda* as a way of demonstrating Iceland and Norway's shared cultural heritage. Snorri's work remains a critical touchpoint for Norse mythology to this day.

Other Sagas

Many other sagas and histories, predominantly Icelandic in origin, exist that point to different aspects of Norse mythology, folklore, and worldview, such as the *Völsunga Saga* and *Gesta Danorum*. While some of these texts mention Norse mythology and paganism, it is not always in a flattering light since they were written post Christianization.

Oral Traditions

Even to this day, remnants of the Norse myths and folklore permeate the oral traditions of Scandinavia and Iceland, circulating through society and people who still practice Norse Paganism.

HOW DO WE DEFINE A "GOD"?

Different cultures have different ways of viewing the world, and that includes how they perceive deities. To know who Freyja is, we need to understand how gods function within Norse cosmology.

As a polytheistic belief system, the Norse cosmology is characterized by the presence of multiple deities. Deities of all religions often have their origins in stories of once-living people and their deeds or grow out of personifications of worldly phenomena such as death, the movement of the sun and the moon, or the activity of volcanoes. But how a culture views their deities—and the kind of relationships they have with them—varies from culture to culture.

Exactly how the Norse people viewed their own deities is tough to pin down. What can be said, however, is that they did not characterize the gods as all-powerful or as having total control over the heavens, the Earth, and fate. The Norse gods were wise and capable, but also extremely human in character, and not immune to making mistakes or being overpowered or outsmarted. They could also die, interestingly enough, although "death" was characterized as "going to a different place" rather than transcending the world or ceasing to exist entirely.

A popular impression people have of deities is that they're rulers or "lords" of certain domains. While this may be true for some pantheons, it's not quite true for the Norse one. Rather, the Norse gods tend to embody the dimensions of life in which they dwell, having been shaped by those things in the same way that people are shaped by the landscapes they have lived in and the experiences they've had. Freyja may be the goddess of love, beauty, war, and magic, but that doesn't make her the ruler or the arbiter of these things for mankind. Instead, she embodies the ways in which women experience themselves.

BLURRY DEFINITIONS

The lines between deity, spirit, and ancestor have a lot of overlap, since all three were venerated in Norse society.

In contemporary Norse Paganism, this is much the same. A "god" is more of a function than a "type" of being, especially since gods can come from many different places and the Norse gods may be referred to by many different titles.

THE TWO FAMILIES OF GODS

The Aesir

The Aesir (pronounced Ah-zir) is the main family of deities within the Norse pantheon. They live in the settlement called Asgard, the name of which comes from the Old Norse *áss*, meaning "[a] god," and *garðr*, which means "dwelling," "farm," or "enclosure." The Aesir can be thought of as a family unit, living in their own settlement. Most of the stories about the gods focus on the exploits and activities of the Aesir. Within the Norse myths, the Aesir and Asgard allegorically represent the idea of people and civilization. Although she was initially part of the Vanir tribe, Freyja is considered part of the Aesir as a result of a hostage exchange during the Aesir–Vanir War, making her a part of both families. Members of the Vanir joining the Aesir may refer allegorically to certain forces in the world—the gentle rains and brilliant sunlight—joining people and society to help build civilization.

The Vanir

The Vanir is a family of deities within Norse cosmology who fought a war with the Aesir in bygone times. The Vanir come from the realm of Vanaheim, which is characterized as lush, green, and mild in weather. The gods from Vanaheim are also characterized as having these qualities, associated as they are with gentle weather and fertility. Freyja and her brother, Frey, and their father, Njord, all belong to the Vanir tribe.

THE NORSE COSMOS

In Norse cosmology, there is not simply one Earth or one heaven, but rather Nine Realms—multiple cosmological worlds, all connected by the branches and roots of the World Tree, Yggdrasil.

1 Asgard **2** Vanaheim **3** Alfheim **4** Midgard **5** Muspelheim **6** Niflheim **7** Jötunheim **8** Nidavellir **9** Svartalfheim

The names of the nine realms are never specifically listed, and the realms that do show up in the *Prose* and *Poetic Edda* tally up to be far more than nine. Nevertheless, a few thinkers have tried to deduce what the Nine Realms might be, if there were, indeed, a canonical nine. Henry Adams Bellows, who translated a version of the *Poetic Edda* in 1923, suggested the following potential list:

Asgard ("the farm of the gods") is the home of the Aesir. It is where many of the gods keep their halls, including Freyja's halls, Sessrumnir and Folkvang. Connecting Asgard to Midgard is the bridge Bifrost, which is represented by the phenomenon of the rainbow.

Vaneheim ("home of the Vanir") is home to the Vanir gods, such as Frey, Freyja, and Njord. Vanaheim is characterized as having lush green lands and mild weather.

Alfheim ("home of the elves") The term "elves" is similar to "fae" in the sense that it's a catch-all for a variety of otherworldly beings. The elves of Alfheim are said to be the *Ljósálfar* or light elves. Alfheim was given to Frey by the gods.

Midgard ("middle Earth") is the tangible world around us—the home of mankind and all the plants and animals that live herein. Midgard is characterized as "an enclosure," a self-contained environment that is simultaneously the abode and the barrier that contains the abode and keeps wild forces such as giants out. In this way Midgard can be thought of a bit like terrarium.

Muspelheim (meaning uncertain) is a primordial world like Niflheim; it's a world of heat and flame. Fire-giants, including Surt, live here. During the creation of the world, Muspelheim was pushed far above Midgard and is kept separate from it via the barrier of the sky. As the sky was being propped up, some sparks escaped Muspelheim and these were fashioned into the stars.

Niflheim ("world of mist") is a cold and misty primordial realm of frost and ice. It is where the sulfuric Elivagar rivers run from the bubbling wellspring, Hverglmir. Niflheim overlaps with Helheim and Niflhel, abodes of the dead. During the creation of Midgard, Niflheim was shoved far below the ground so that it would not freeze the world.

Jötunheim ("giant country") is the home of the giants. It is mountainous, wild, and inaccessible by usual means; the gods often have to make their way across bodies of water or fly by means of magic to reach it.

Nidavellir ("dark downward country") is the home of the dwarves, master craftsmen and smiths. Nidavellir may be an abode within Svartalfheim or they may be one and the same. It is also called Myrkheim, or "dark abode."

Svartalfheim ("world of the black elves") is the home of the *Dökkálfar*, the dark elves who live beneath the earth and have a nature quite unlike that of their light-elf counterparts. The gods visited Svartalfheim to acquire Gleipnir, the fetter made of impossible things that was used to bind Fenrir, the giant wolf.

VANAHEIM

Though Freyja's halls are in Asgard and she resides there with the Aesir, Vanaheim is her home realm and reflects her association with beauty and fertility.

Vanaheim is the home of the Vanir and depicted as a lush, green abode with brilliant skies and mild weather. The Vanir themselves are said to bring the properties of this realm with them, thus blessing our human realm of Midgard. We can see this in Freyja's family members. Njord, her father, presides over the sea and is prayed to for good weather and easy voyages. Frey, her brother, is associated with fertility, springtime, and blooming flowers. Freyja herself is compared to sunlight, particularly brilliant, golden rays.

Since Vanaheim is described as a lush, green place, it's sometimes linked to Ireland. As the Norse facilitated trade with their neighbors, the Celts, it is possible that the island inspired the descriptions of Vanaheim. This is similar to how the inhabitable mountains of Scandinavia inspired Jötunheim, the settled farmland areas inspired Asgard, and the frozen north inspired the underworld of Helheim. This has also led people to wonder if the Aesir–Vanir War describes a conflict between the Norse people and the Celts, and whether Freyja may have originally been a Celtic figure.

There could be another reason, though. The animistic beliefs of the Norse support the idea that the different worlds in Norse cosmology are "astral" planes that are reflected in Midgard; that when we look at wildfires, frozen wastelands, or green fields, we are looking at emanations of Muspelheim, Helheim, and Vanaheim, respectively. These things are the essences of these worlds, overlapping with our own reality.

This would mean that Vanaheim reveals itself whenever certain conditions are present; for example, during a summer rain shower or on golden afternoons when the light hits in such a way that everything looks brilliant.

If Asgard represents civilization where humans live, and Jötunheim hostile wilds where humans cannot live, then Vanaheim represents something in between: gentle nature. This is where the natural forces that benefit mankind come from, such as the rain and sunshine that allow us to farm and grow food.

THE NORSE ENTITIES

Norse mythology and Scandinavian folklore are filled with a number of beings. Many of these tend to be non-taxonomical in nature, and some may blend in with others. Here is a selection of the many different entities that are commonly mentioned in the stories.

NORNIR

The *Nornir*, or the Norns, are female deities who shape the course of fate and destiny. The key three are called Urd, Verdandi, and Skuld, whose names mean "became," "becoming," and "shall be." They have a well at the base of Yggdrasil from which they draw sacred water. This they pour on Yggdrasil to rejuvenate it. Other Norns were thought to exist and visit newborns to determine their future.

VALKYRJUR

Valkyrjur or valkyries are the women who ride over the battlefields and carry fallen warriors to Sessrumnir and Valhalla after they die. The word valkyrie means "chooser of the slain." Valkyries are sometimes depicted riding horses or transforming into birds, and they have their own stories in the Old Norse sagas.

EINHERJAR

Einherjar are the warriors who die in battle and are then chosen for Odin's hall. The *einherjar* feast and skirmish until Odin calls on them to fight during Ragnarok. The word *einherjar* literally means "army of one" or "those who fight alone."

ALVAR

Alvar is the term for elves, and they are depicted in many ways. There are the light elves who live in bright, heavenly planes and the dark elves who live deep in the earth—these may or may not be the same as dwarves. They are sometimes characterized as tall and sometimes small.

WIGHTS

"Wight" is a general term for "spirit," and can refer to any sort of entity in general. It comes from the Old Norse word, *vættr*.

LANDVÆTTIR

Landvættir are land spirits, beings who embody or personify a specific landscape or environment. The land itself is the spirit's corporeal form.

NISSE/TOMTE

Nisse or *tomte* are house spirits, a bit like brownies or gnomes, who are thought to relate to the luck and prosperity of the home. Not all homes were thought to have a *nisse*, but if one moved in, it was important to make sure it was happy and included in the goings-on of domestic life. Part of that involved keeping the house tidy and leaving offerings of porridge (with added butter) by the fire for them.

TROLLS

While characterized in fairy tales as creatures with cow tails that turn to stone in sunlight, trolls as spirits have a much broader definition. In the Scandinavian languages, *troll* denotes anything that is "other," and the word has connotations of magic and sorcery. Trolls may take on a number of appearances: boulders, cats, people, non-corporeal beings, and more. What makes something a troll has to do with the quality it possesses, rather than its physical appearance. Trolls in many ways are similar to *jötnar*.

VÖLUR

Völva (plural: *völur*) is the Old Norse word for witch, seeress, or wise woman, and means "staff bearer." *Völur* would have practiced a kind of magic known as seid (Old Norse *seiðr*), used for prophecies, portents, and otherworldly travel. The word *spákona*, meaning literally "prophecy woman," was used interchangeably with *völva*.

JÖTNAR

Jötnar (singular: *jötun*) are beings who embody the wild, untameable landscapes and forces of the world. They dwell in places where people can potentially visit, but can't permanently live in—in extreme heat, in extreme cold, on the peaks of frozen mountains, in the hearts of volcanoes, in the depths of the ocean, in the depths of winter, and so on. Their realm is called Jötunheim.

Jötnar are referred to as "giants" in English, though they are not always large in stature. Rather, their "giant" nature comes from the energy of their presence, which feels wild, unrefined, and big. If people are like polished jewels, then *jötnar* are like raw ores. Many of the Norse gods are *jötun* or part-*jötun*.

THURS

Thurs are giants who represent forces actively hostile toward human life—volcanic eruptions, rockslides, avalanches, and so on. The hostility of these forces is allegorically represented as "a hatred for humans" in the Norse myths. While typical giants can potentially be sociable, this is not true of the thurs.

The word "thurs" comes from the Old Norse word *hrímþursar* which is often translated as "frost-giant." But just as *jötun* doesn't really mean "a large humanoid," *hrímþursar* doesn't really mean "a large humanoid frost-elemental." The implications are more along the lines of "the hostile forces that dwell at the frozen edges of the world."

Terms like "frost-giant" and "fire-giant" denote the environment the giant lives in, rather than different types of giants.

DVERGR

Dvergr or dwarves are said to live deep beneath the earth. They are characterized as masters of craftwork, particularly when it comes to smithing enchanted or impossible objects. The dwarves are responsible for creating some of the most exceptional treasures belonging to the Aesir, including Freyja's necklace (see page 37).

DÍSIR

Dísir (singular: *dís*), anglicized to disir, are female deities connected with the supernatural. They were worshipped in fertility rites and appeared with warlike or hostile attitudes in Eddic poetry. They are also associated with death and come to take those whose time it is to die. They are sometimes thought of as spirit-guardians who protect warriors.

CHAPTER 2:

WHO IS FREYJA?

There's a great deal more to Freyja, the goddess of love, magic, and war, than just her key attributes. Freyja is dynamic, tough, clever, courageous, and extremely well versed in the mysteries of life. In this chapter, we discuss who Freyja is, what she is like, and her main characteristics, and learn about her family and important relations.

FREYJA'S NAME

Freyja's name simply means "the lady," which is thought by scholars to be a byname for the goddess rather than her real name. If Freyja was known by any other name, then this has since been lost to time.

Freyja's name in Old Norse comes from the old Proto-Germanic word *frawjōn*, which also means "lady" or "mistress." This root word is where we derive the modern German word "*frau*," meaning "woman," "Mrs." or "Ms."

However, Freyja is sometimes referred to by other names within extant sources of Norse mythology. Some of these names are as follows:

Gef ("the giver"): A name attributed to Freyja, Gef means "she who gives prosperity and happiness," but it is also connected to the goddess Gefjun (who is associated with oxen and plowing).

Horn (potentially "flaxen"): A name of unknown origins connected to the goddess Freyja. It's found in a few different Swedish place names.

Mardoll ("one who illuminates the sea" or "one who makes the sea swell"): A name of uncertain etymology, Mardoll is possibly related to Freyja's father, Njord, a god associated with the sea and sailors. The name also occurs as a kenning (a poetic turn-of-phrase) for "gold" in skaldic poetry (a type of Old Norse verse).

Skjalf ("shaker"): The name of a daughter of a Finnish king, although the *Prose Edda* also attributes this to Freyja. Both figures share similar necklace imagery.

Syr ("sow"): A name attributed to Freyja. Pigs and boars were important to the Vanir deities. Sacrifices of pigs were made in honor of both Freyja and her brother, Frey, in ancient times.

Throng and Thrungva ("throng"): Two names for Freyja where the context has been lost with time.

Vanadis ("the dís of the Vanir"): *Dís* (singular) and *dísir* (plural) are female supernatural beings or minor goddesses that give or withhold life, protection, and prosperity (see page 21).

Valfreyja ("lady of the slain"): A kenning that refers to Freyja's role as a warrior and psychopomp (someone who guides souls into the afterlife).

FREYJA'S PERSONALITY

Since Freyja is only in the spotlight during brief moments in the Norse myths, much of what is said and known about her personality comes from how she's experienced by those who venerate her.

TENACIOUS AND RESOLUTE

In the Norse myths and as a pagan goddess worshipped in the modern day, Freyja is characterized by her tenacious, resolute nature. To put it another way, she has great strength of will and the determination to get things done. She can, however, be stubborn at times, but not necessarily to her detriment. For example, in her myths, Freyja vehemently opposes exchanging her hand in marriage as payment for Asgard's wall (see *Freyja Escapes Marriage*, pages 62–65). She also rejected the same request when it came to exchanging her for Thor's hammer, Mjolnir, which had been stolen by a *jötun* for the purpose of this bribery (see *The Theft of Thor's Hammer*, pages 72–75).

The trait of tenacity encompasses a constellation of different facets of Freyja's character. She's someone who is determined, someone who knows how to advocate, and someone who, at times, can be like the girl who digs her feet in the dirt because she's already made up her mind what she wants. That's Freyja.

CUNNING AND CLEVER

Freyja's cunning and intelligence are made clear in Norse mythology. These words suggest "someone who knows how to use knowledge skillfully," rather than simply meaning smart or witty. Freyja demonstrates her cleverness by tricking Hyndla into disclosing the family lineage of her lover, Ottar (see *Freyja Rides with Hyndla*, pages 76–79).

Freyja can be called upon for help in all matters that require crafty thinking, or whenever we're trying to piece something together. She's especially good at this when it comes to navigating outcomes or orchestrating results.

WISE

Freyja, much like her older counterpart Frigg, is very wise. She can offer advice and insight into the mysteries of all things, ranging from women's issues to the design of the universe. However, her advice and counsel can just as easily apply to smaller and more personal conundrums. Even Odin seeks out Freyja's wisdom at times.

PROTECTIVE

Freyja is an inherently protective force. While not as "motherly" as Frigg, anyone under Freyja's care is fiercely and loyally protected. She can be like a mother bear or sister bear when it comes to her charges, and will do all she can to make sure they're guarded against harm, should this pose a risk.

This protective energy also extends to simple support in life. Freyja can be like a sister or aunt who provides advice, wisdom, pep talks, and general encouragement in all matters of life. For those who choose to work with

her in this capacity, she can encourage us to make good decisions in romantic affairs, help us achieve happiness in partnerships, and will do her best to protect us from domestic violence.

Freyja is also a protector-guardian of cats, so she can also be called upon to help with feline-related pet needs.

PATIENT

Like the rest of the Norse gods, Freyja is very patient with her devotees. She doesn't get angry if they forget to give offerings, nor does she make demands of them. Like all deities, she wants to see us thriving and doing well, and she will interact with someone at their own pace.

COURAGEOUS

Courage runs in the veins of the Norse gods, but this is especially so with Freyja. The word "courage" comes from the French word *coeur*, meaning "heart," so this is more than just a show of bravery—courage is the circumstance of having passion and care to the point that it can drive us to overcome the state of fear.

Take care to remember that courage is not the act of being fearless; rather it is the act of being afraid but having the resolve to do something anyway. And Freyja excels in helping us to overcome this fear. After all, she's a warrior who fights passionately for what's right, and she can likewise teach the warrior's spirit—even for those whose flame was extinguished long ago.

CREATIVE

As well as being wise and clever, Freyja is also very creative. Her sort of creativity is a little different to simply having artistic talent. Rather, it describes the state of being adaptive and innovative to the point of artistry. The ability to create goes hand in hand with the ability to shape outcomes—both are important for the art known as seid (see page 34), which is something Freyja specializes in. She is delighted by acts of creativity, which makes them especially good as offerings to her.

STRONG AND POWERFUL

A friend of mine once described Freyja as being "an iron fist in a velvet glove." I've found this to be a great description of her power as a goddess. Freyja is a mighty figure in a multitude of ways, from physical to magical to personal. She has the type of strength that comes from deep within rather than one that stems from imitating might or bravado.

Freyja can be called upon when strength is needed in challenging times, or when we find it difficult to summon strength within ourselves.

TEMPESTUOUS

Freyja can be a force to reckon with for anyone who makes an enemy of her. Such a response takes effort, so don't worry too much about being on the receiving end of her wrath. However, if someone goes out of their way and truly insults what she stands for, then they will find themselves at the mercy of her anger.

GOOD SENSE OF HUMOR

Despite everything, Freyja is blessed with a good sense of humor, and she's not particularly tense or stern in most circumstances. She enjoys lively banter in good company—although perhaps unlike the god Loki, what Frejya finds humorous is more selective.

FREYJA'S APPEARANCE

Freyja is said to be the most beautiful of the Norse goddesses. She's often shown wearing her necklace Brisingamen and accompanied by two cats. Other times she's depicted as a warrior goddess or crying tears of red-gold as she pines for her missing husband.

Beyond her beauty, there's no definitive description of Freyja anywhere. Historical artifacts often show her with a necklace around her neck or flanked by cats. She's also linked to artifacts depicting a woman with a wand or staff, but it's less certain whether this is Freyja or not.

More contemporary depictions began appearing around the 1800s, when interest in Norse studies grew and the gods reappeared in popular culture. During this time, Freyja was often correlated with the Greek Aphrodite or Roman Venus, and portrayed in a similar way to these ancient goddesses. Nowadays depictions of Freyja have become more diverse. She's sometimes shown as fat, sometimes thin, and sometimes older or younger, and often portrayed in all her different aspects, not just as a beautiful, young damsel.

Freyja values giving women who call on her the chance to see themselves reflected in her, so how she looks can change depending on the viewer. She may also take on the appearance of what we find most beautiful about women—and specifically *beautiful*, as opposed to merely physically attractive. This may not always be what we anticipate.

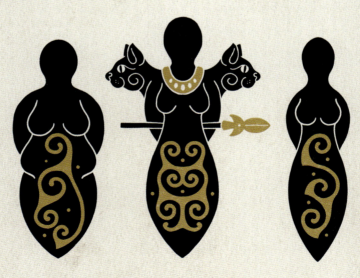

FREYJA'S CHARACTERISTICS

In previous pages we looked at Freyja's personality and shifting appearance. Here, we will explore some of her characteristics that define who she is to the Norse people.

VANIR

Freyja (along with her brother, Frey, and her father Njord) was originally from the Vanir tribe. After the Aesir–Vanir War (see pages 60–61), the three of them were exchanged as hostages in an agreement with the Aesir, who traded two of their own in return: Hoenir and Mimir. Freyja, along with her brother and father, carry attributes that are linked to the Vanir, including associations with mild weather and fertile landscapes.

Freyja is arguably of two worlds now: firstly, her homeland of Vanaheim and, secondly, her adopted family, the Aesir.

WARRIOR

Just like her father, Njord, and her brother Frey, Freyja is a skilled warrior. Whenever there was a battle, she would ride into the thick of the skirmish along with the valkyries. Odin was so impressed with Freyja's prowess in battle that he gave her first pick of souls who fell in battle. So, while half the fallen warriors went to Odin, Freyja could have first choice of the other half.

Unfortunately, there aren't many surviving legends of Freyja in battle. Indeed, most of her battle exploits are known from oral traditions rather than any of the Icelandic sagas.

SEERESS/VÖLVA

Freyja is characterized as a talented *völva*, a word that means "seeress/staff-bearer/witch/wise woman." This was a recognized profession in Norse societies, and one that was mostly held by women. Wise women often wandered from place to place to provide their services, which ranged from giving prophecies and telling fortunes, to conversing with the dead, to addressing matters of fate and outcomes.

Similarly, Freyja is also portrayed as a *seiðkona*, which broadly means "a woman who practices magic/seid." Seid (or *seiðr* in Old Norse) was a methodology for seeing trends and patterns or cause and effect, and for shaping future outcomes based on these trends.

Lastly, Freyja is also considered to be a *spåkona*, or a woman who makes prophecies. Some scholars believe that it was Freyja who foretold Ragnarok in the *Völuspá* (found in the *Poetic Edda*), channeling the memories of the dead.

FREYJA'S ASSOCIATIONS

While the Norse deities aren't lords or ladies of any domains, it would be a lie to say that they don't have any associations. When necessary, they can be called upon for guidance and advice when the issue concerns their specialties. Freyja's associations are given here.

BEAUTY

Freyja is deeply associated with beauty, and in the Norse myths she's often coveted by various giants because of her extraordinary beauty. Although this is something of a ruse for the sake of the plot of the myths, Freyja's connection with, and understanding of, beauty is very real. She can be called upon for advice regarding what beauty is, what it means, or how to promote it in one's life. She's especially helpful when it comes to building self-esteem around personal appearance, and will help reframe ideas about what it means to be beautiful.

FERTILITY

Along with beauty, Freyja is also linked to fertility. This attribute is something she shares with the rest of the Vanir, and she can therefore help with matters pertaining to sex, pregnancy, menstruation, and reproductive health. She can be called upon for assistance with conceiving children, or likewise with preventing conception. As well as personal fertility, Freyja is also associated with the fertility of the land, and can bring mild weather and verdant growth to places that need it.

WEALTH

Since Freyja is associated with fertility, she's also, by extension, linked to wealth. The state of wealth is more than just the state of having money—it's also the state of abundance in our lives, which comes as a result of fertile conditions.

Wealth is something we create in our lives through effort. Maintaining good social relations creates a wealth of connections and friendships. Maintaining good grooming habits, eating good food, and exercising well create a wealth of health and beauty. Cultivating personal awareness and honesty creates a wealth of discernment and wisdom. Taking care of the spaces around us and making sure they're thriving creates a wealthy environment. And, of course, making good financial decisions and learning to tap into the flow of money creates financial wealth.

The creation of wealth is considered part of seid, the magic in which Freyja specializes. If any area of your life feels as if it's lacking in any way, Freyja can give you the tools you need to create abundance there.

LOVE

Freyja is associated with love in all its forms; sexual love, romantic love, the love between family, platonic love, and more. All forms of love are within Freyja's wheelhouse, and she can help people find love or explore different types of love.

Young love and romance are of especial interest to Freyja. She can help with matchmaking, choosing partners, or

finding someone compatible. She can also assist with love-related troubles, difficulties, or questions.

WAR

While Freyja is known as the goddess of love, magic, and beauty, she's also recognized as the goddess of war. This might be war in the traditional sense, but it can also refer to any situation where we find ourselves in a position of conflict. She can help us fight personal battles or any circumstance where the odds seem to be working against us.

Since she is a goddess of war, Freyja is also a goddess of defense and protection. This is particularly true for children, and she can be called upon to safeguard them in times of need.

DEATH

With war comes death. The Norse view of death was very different from our own, though; death was not considered the opposite of life, but one of life's vital functions. They believed that those who passed away could still involve themselves in people's lives, even long after they were gone, and so the dead were called upon for advice, guidance, and protection when needed.

Freyja is associated with death in that she oversees the souls of the slain. She can act as a psychopomp—a spirit that guides between this life and the hereafter—for those who fall in battle. She's also able to consult with the dead in her capacity as a seeress.

SEID AND MAGIC

Freyja is associated with magic of all sorts, and particularly the varieties known and practiced in Norse society. First and foremost among these is seid. As mentioned earlier, seid is the practice of looking at the movement patterns of circumstance to predict future outcomes. This web of circumstances is known as the Web of Wyrd, with the word "wyrd" referring to the overall "design" of circumstances created through the interactions of cause and effect.

Those who practice seid can not only predict the future, but also shape it by altering current circumstances and environments. Through this "weaving" of the wyrd, we can shape destiny itself.

The Norse believed in destiny, and were of the mind that we inherited the trajectory of the destinies our ancestors traveled upon—for example, someone from a family of farmers was likely to be a farmer, while someone from a royal family was destined to continue that royal line; family lines riddled with conflict would continue in this way into the next generation, and efforts to improve the family culture would also be reflected in the family wyrd.

But the Norse people didn't believe in predestination, or the idea that our lives are already written for us; nothing about the future is fixed or set in stone. Even Odin, the Allfather, had to learn to shape the otherwise free design of the wyrd to orchestrate outcomes.

This ability to shape outcomes and determine the trends of the future is a characteristic Freyja also shares with a goddess named Frigg, Odin's wife, who may be a more elderly version of Freyja. The two goddesses also share another magical characteristic: Both own a

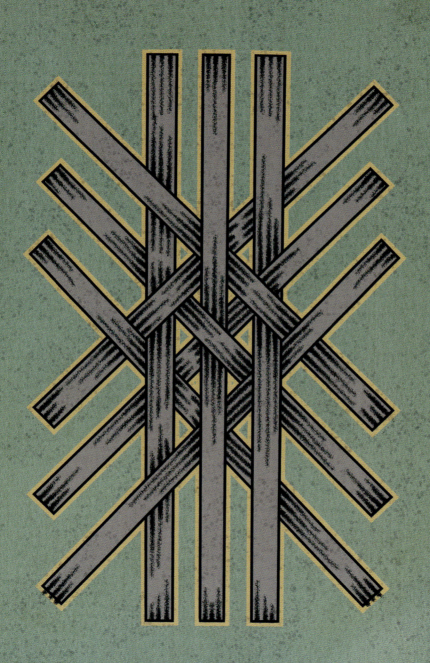

"falcon skin" that they use to transform themselves into birds and fly around the world. These skins are sometimes portrayed as cloaks of feathers. At one point in the Norse myths, Freyja lends her feathered cloak to Loki, so he can fly to Jötunheim to discover who stole Mjolnir (see *The Theft of Thor's Hammer*, pages 72–75). Given the motifs in this story, we can deduce that the "falcon skin" is an allegory for the shamanic practice of astral-projection or astral-travel.

For any questions regarding magic, Freyja can be called upon for advice, assistance, and instruction.

GIRLHOOD, WOMANHOOD, FEMININITY

Freyja is associated with femininity in the same way that her brother, Frey, is associated with masculinity. While we don't exactly know how the Norse people viewed femininity, we can reasonably assume it was similar to how we view it in the modern day—where there are many different interpretations of what this means. Freyja represents them all, ranging from traditional to non-traditional expressions.

Freyja's function in Norse society was likely similar to that of Barbie or Wonder Woman in that she served as both a role model for women and girls, but also as a figure defined by and for women and girls. Since Freyja is a goddess, she also represents those aspects of being female favored by humanity.

Gender is not always as important to one god's self-expression as it is to another's, but it is for Freyja. She never expects her followers to adopt the same view of themselves—everyone is their own person, after all—but Freyja puts gender at the center of who she is. Naturally, you don't have to be a woman to work with Freyja. But Freyja has a way of broadening our definition of being female and can help us understand what it means, regardless of our own sex or gender. She can help us cultivate a deeper understanding and appreciation of being female.

FALCONS

Falcons are sleek, midsize birds of prey known for their fast flight and sharp beaks. They can also operate as messengers of Freyja—possibly being the goddess herself in disguise. Freyja's feathered cloak allows her to cast her awareness into other worlds, including our material plane Midgard. The appearance of Freyja in this way can be abrupt and significant. If the goddess is appearing to us, it's to get our attention.

NOTABLE POSSESSIONS

A few items specific to Freyja are mentioned in the Norse myths.

BRISINGAMEN

Brisingamen, or *Brísingamen* in Old Norse, is the name of Freyja's beautiful necklace. The name means "the gleaming fire-amber (decorative) neck-torc" or more colloquially, "the beautiful necklace of fiery amber." This word evokes the way amber shines in the light, giving us an insight into what Freyja's necklace probably looks like; it glows spectacularly in the same way as amber, and perhaps it even uses amber in its construction.

Amber is intimately associated with Freyja because she cries tears of red-gold for her lost and wandering husband, Od. But this red-gold is not a reference to the gold and copper alloy we call "red-gold" today, for this metal was not around in Norse society. Instead, "red-gold" is a poetic reference to the amber found abundantly in the Baltic Sea (the connection of amber to the sea is similar to Freyja's connection with her father Njord, who personifies the sea and the weather fronts upon it).

If the Norse people ever made dolls for their children, it's easy to imagine how this beautiful and abundant material, amber, could have been used to create necklaces for them. From there, the imaginations of children would have given the necklace a mythology of its own.

The surviving myth of how Freyja got her necklace is somewhat skewed by post-Christianized influences, but like many of the magical things owned by the Norse gods, this necklace was crafted by the dwarves (see *The Forging of Brisingamen*, page 67).

CHARIOT PULLED BY CATS

Freyja is said to ride in a chariot pulled by two cats. These cats are unnamed, although there is later speculation regarding their names (see *Freyja and Cats*, pages 40–41), so it's not known what significance they may have for Freyja. But we do know that this motif was a popular one.

CLOAK OF FEATHERS

Freyja is said to have a "falcon skin" that lets her travel to far-off domains. This is often interpreted as a cloak made of feathers that transforms her into a falcon. However, the "falcon skin" may, in fact, be a reference to a specific kind of shamanic ability. Freyja once loaned her feathered cloak to Loki, so he could fly to Jötunheim and locate Thor's missing hammer, which was stolen by a giant (see *The Theft of Thor's Hammer*, pages 72–75). When Freyja travels to Midgard, she sometimes does so in the guise of a falcon, donning her feathered cloak so she can fly.

FREYJA AND FLOWERS

Freyja's association with love and fertility begets a connection with spring and summer, and nothing represents these months more than flowers. For this reason, flower associations have found their way into modern veneration practices for Freyja.

SNOWDROP

One folktale goes like this: Freyja was very sad when she first came to Asgard. Compared to the lush, green landscape of Vanaheim, her new home was cold and gray. One day she cried, missing the flowers from home, but when her tears hit the earth, beautiful white flowers sprang up in their place. In some versions of this story, the flower is the snowdrop, but in others it's lily of the valley.

COWSLIP

Cowslips are beautiful little flowers of red and gold, sometimes referred to as the Virgin Mary's keys. However, their Swedish name is *gullviva*, which potentially means "gold woman." We know from other examples that the Virgin Mary's name replaced the names of plants once associated with Frigg and Freyja, making it likely that this "gold woman" was originally a reference to Freyja. The mention of keys also lends itself to a connection with Freyja due to the role they played in Norse marriages; the bride would be presented with the keys to the house during her wedding to indicate that she was now the owner of the home.

COLUMBINE

In Swedish folklore, the columbine flower is associated with Freyja, perhaps on account of its supposed status as an aphrodisiac. It was thought that ingesting columbine as a potion or tincture would promote fertility in brides. However, columbine is mildly toxic and so shouldn't be eaten right off the plant. Growing some columbines in a flower bed or container would make a wonderful offering to Freyja.

DAISY

Daisies are sacred to both Freyja and to Balder, the shining god. These small flowers were given to warriors for good luck, making them a good charm of protection from Freyja. They can also symbolize new beginnings, motherhood, and childbirth, which are all within Freyja's purview.

HEMP

Naturally, it's important to check the legality of hemp within your location because it cannot be grown everywhere. However, in places where it can, hemp is strongly associated with Freyja, on account of the fact that cannabis was used by *völur* (see page 21) within the context of their practices.

FREYJA AND CATS

In Norse mythology, Freyja has a chariot pulled by two cats. Nothing else is said about them in the Norse myths other than this. Their scant mention and mysterious nature has led to a lot of speculation about these cats, such as what they're like, where they come from, and what their relationship to Freyja is.

A Russian tale, based on Norse mythology, tells the story of how Freyja first got her two cats:

Once upon a time, Thor was out fishing when he heard a wonderful sound that lulled him to sleep. But just as he drifted off, a noise woke him once more. Irritated, he went to search for the source and came across a cat named Bayun and two blue kittens. The kittens, both male, were sleeping soundly while Bayun was singing to them.

Thor asked the cat if he was the father of the two kittens, and Bayun replied that he was. He then explained that he had met a pretty lady-cat in the spring and together they had had two kittens, but their mother had left and now he was stuck raising the kittens by himself.

Bayun asked Thor for help, and Thor made up his mind to give the kittens to Freyja. Once the matter was settled, Bayun turned into a bird and flew away, while Thor gathered up the kittens to take back to Asgard. Those two cats grew up to be strong animals that pulled Freyja's chariot.

In the mid-1980s, the writer Diana L. Paxton gave the cats the names Tregul ("tree-gold," referring to amber) and Bygul ("bee-gold," referring to honey).

Further stories have cropped up about these cats, including one that describes how Freyja and her cats rescue Frey after he is kidnapped by the giant Thjazi. The story begins with Frey refusing to hand over his magnificent sword to Thjazi. Angry at this, the giant turns into an eagle and snatches up Frey with his talons, carrying him off to Jötunheim. Hearing this, Freyja jumps into her chariot, and she and her cats ride swiftly over the land. Using their keen eyes and exceptional instincts, the two felines find Thjazi's lair and Freyja comes to her brother's rescue. Frey escapes unharmed.

Though these legends may be newer, Freyja's connection with cats is much older. Cats played a role in Norse weddings, known as handfastings. A newly wed bride would be given a kitten as a bridal gift to help protect the home, keep pests away, and look after the children. Cats may have come to be associated with Freyja in this way because she's also the goddess associated with love, marriage, and conception. As the kitten was presented specifically to the bride, it was thus intimately associated with Freyja.

Cats are also connected to Freyja in the form of the *trollkatt*, a feline who operates as a witch's familiar. Most of the medieval folklore surrounding trollkatts depicts them as mischievous milk-thieves, but all these associations point to a much older connection to Freyja and potentially Frigg.

Since cats are effectively Freyja's charges, they also sometimes act as her messengers. Depending on the context, the appearance of a cat, especially one that is new and unfamiliar, can be an auspicious sign. Sometimes, the cat might even be a gift from the goddess herself.

The cat in the Russian story seems to be a breed of cat known as the Russian Blue, which has a dense, shimmery gray coat. However, the type of cat the Norse people probably gifted each other might have looked more similar to the Norwegian Forest Cat. These are large, regal mammals that are well-suited to Scandinavian climates. They have dense coats, large paws, and arboreal hunting habits. But despite their size and stature, these cats are exceptionally patient, easily tolerating the antics of children and happy to receive snuggles and pets at any moment. They may have also accompanied people as they sat spinning and weaving around the fire, giving them an association with seid (see *Seid and Practicing Seid*, pages 103–109). This may echo our modern image of the witch's cat, a familiar who accompanies a woman as she's performing spells and witchcraft.

FREYJA AND THE DÍSIR

One of Freyja's names is *Vanadís* ("the dís of the Vanir"). *Dís* (singular) and *dísir* (plural) refer to a collective of goddesses as well as to women connected with the supernatural.

In Eddic poetry, *dísir*—anglicized to disir—appear with warlike or hostile attitudes and as helpers in childbirth. They are also associated with death. The same picture meets us in different sagas—for example, in the heroic tale of *Ásmundar saga kappabana* ("Asmund the Champion-Killer"), where on the eve of battle the hero dreams about armed women, known as *spádísir*, who promise to protect him and follow him as guardian spirits during his adventures.

King Sigmundr in the *Völsunga saga* ("Saga of the Völsungs") is similarly protected by his *spádísir* until Odin intervenes. Belief in the guardian disir is also reflected in *Hálfs saga* ("The Saga of Half"), where one of the fighting men evokes his disir and his enemy answers: "*Yðr munu dauðar dísir állar,*" or "All your disir may be dead," implying the failure of the attack.

The purpose of the *dísablót* ("the sacrifice to the disir") and *álfablót* ("the sacrifice to the elves") was undoubtedly that of promoting fertility. Since Frey was the recipient of the *álfablót*, due to his association with Alfheim, it seems permissible to assume that the *dísablót* was devoted to Freyja, the *Vanadís*. The rituals were probably performed by both men and women but directed to Frey and Freyja, respectively.

The *dísablót* took place in "the winter nights"—that is, at the beginning of October, according to *Víga-Glúms saga* ("The Saga of Viga-Glum") and *Egils saga Skallagrímssonar* ("Egil's Saga").

Like the Vanir, the disir were worshipped in fertility rites that took place in fall and spring, perhaps coinciding with the autumnal and vernal equinoxes. It is also evident that the disir, like the Vanir, were bearers of the chthonic function (meaning they were linked to the underworld), since they were connected with the earth and the year's crop. Their cult belonged to the family and household and involved secret rites, such as the reddening of the *hörg*, or sacrificial altar.

FREYJA'S FAMILY AND IMPORTANT RELATIONS

Freyja has many key people in her life, some of whom she calls family, and others who remain important to her despite a lack of relationship between them.

From left: Hildisvini, Frey, Skadi, Njord's sister, Od, Freyja

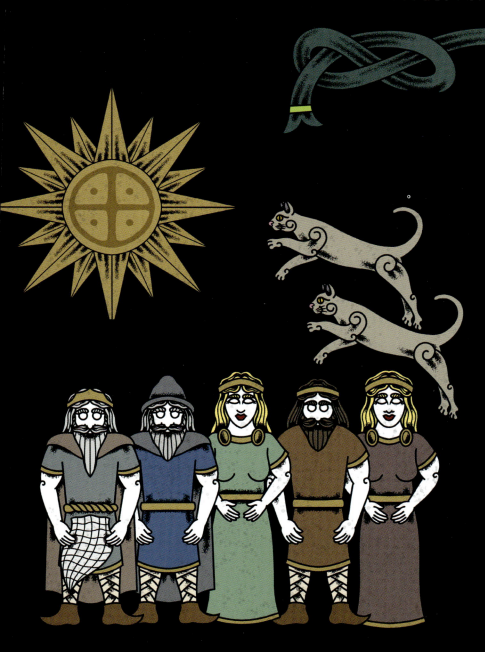
From left: Njord, Odin, Hnoss, Ottar, Gersemi, Cats

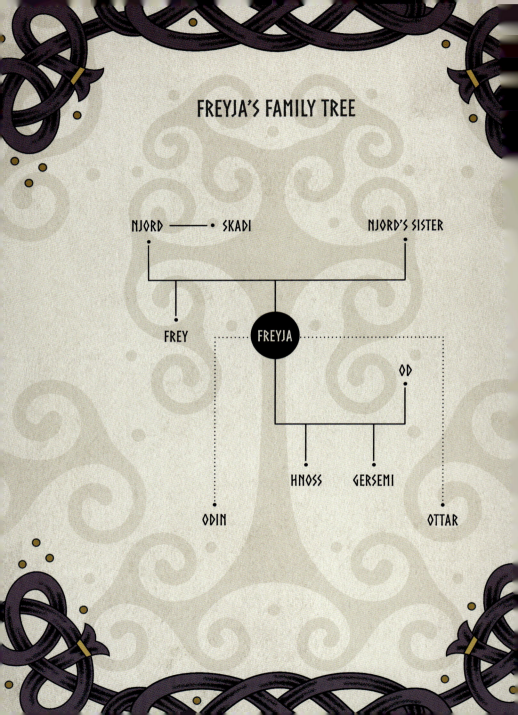

NJORD

Njord is Freyja's father, who personifies the sea and the weather fronts that exist upon it. He's associated with sailors and seafaring, and can be prayed to for good winds and safe travels while out at sea. Njord's hall is called Noatun (or *Nóatún* in Old Norse), which means "ship enclosure." Perhaps his "hall" is none other than the cabins of ships.

NJORD'S SISTER

When Njord was with the Vanir, he had a relationship with his unnamed sister, and she gave birth to the twins Freyja and Frey as a result. This incestuous behavior was permitted by the Vanir, but forbidden among the Aesir. This may be because the Vanir represent the "gentle forces of nature" and can therefore intermingle freely with one another. But since the Aesir represent "people and society," this wouldn't work for them.

Very little is known about Njord's sister-wife. She could perhaps be the Germanic goddess Nerthus, a goddess only attested to by the Roman lawmaker Tacitus. Nerthus is a feminine name that shares the same root as Njord's, but it's unclear if Nerthus is a separate figure in and of herself, or Njord in a female aspect.

SKADI

Freyja's step-mother is Skadi (*Skaði* in Old Norse), a *jötun* associated with winter. After Skadi's father was killed by the Aesir, she marched to Asgard to demand compensation for his death. The compensation she asked for in return was marriage to the shining and beautiful god, Balder, but due to feats of trickery, she ended up marrying Njord instead.

Njord and Skadi have an uneasy marriage. He enjoys the ocean, with its waves and seagulls, while she prefers the peaks of mountains, with their snow and frost. Neither could adapt to the other's climate. This might be an allegory for the geography of parts of Scandinavia, where tall mountains suddenly meet the seas, thanks to the long and winding fjords.

FREY

Freyja's twin brother is a god named Frey, or *Freyr* in Old Norse. Just as Freyja represents the feminine aspect of life, so Frey represents the masculine one. He's associated with soft rains and skies bursting with light, and is known for bringing fertility to the land come springtime. He rides on a golden boar named Gullinbursti, who has bristles made of gold that shine so brightly they're blinding to look at.

Frey is a skilled warrior, but for all his skills he decided to trade away his sword for his wife, Gerd. This turned out to be an unwise decision, for he had to fight with a stag antler instead when Ragnarok began.

HNOSS

Freyja's daughter with Od, Hnoss is so beautiful that all things precious are named after her. Her name means "treasure" or "gem," but is also similar to other Scandinavian words that mean "sweetheart" or "infant." The multiple implications behind this word suggests that Hnoss represents the feeling mothers have for their newborns.

GERSEMI

Gersemi is another of Freyja's daughters. Like Hnoss, her name means "treasure" or "jewel." It might be Gersemi is just another name for Hnoss, and they're the same person, but they could also be sisters or even twins.

OD

Od (or *Óðr* in Old Norse) is the name of Freyja's absent husband. The word "Od" is a reference to "mind, sense, soul, wit, feeling," but also to "song, poetry." The fact that Od is always off wandering is a metaphor for the wandering mind. Freyja cries tears of red-gold (amber) in his absence, and dons various disguises to visit the material world and look for him.

Just as Freyja is in some ways a youthful version of Frigg (who represents older womanhood), so Od may be a youthful version of Odin. The fact that Od and Odin's names both share the same root suggests the two figures share a close connection, even if they're not one and the same.

OTTAR
While Freyja has taken (and continues to take) many lovers, one of these was a man named Ottar. Freyja helps him discover his unknown lineage. To do this, she disguises him as a giant boar, and the two ride with a giantess called Hyndla, who knows all ancestries. Ottar listens silently while Hyndla rattles off the members of his family line.

HILDISVINI
Boars were sacred to the Vanir. Like her brother Frey, Freyja has a giant boar she uses as a steed; its name is Hildisvini (or *Hildisvíni* in Old Norse), which means "battle swine." While far less is written about Freyja's boar compared to Frey's, we can assume from his name that he was a battle animal, perhaps even one she rides into war.

ODIN
Odin is the chief of the Aesir gods and carries the title "Allfather." He's motivated by a powerful thirst for knowledge and stops at nothing to understand the deeper mysteries of life. After Freyja was exchanged as a hostage during the Aesir–Vanir War, she taught Odin the secrets of seid, likely at his request. Odin is also sometimes depicted as one of Freyja's lovers; in later medieval stories, she's characterized as one of Odin's concubines.

CATS
Freyja has two cats to draw her chariot. There is little mention of them in the surviving myths, so what we know comes from later tales. They're thought to be gray males.

FREYJA AND FRIGG

Freyja has a lot in common with the goddess Frigg. While the two figures are treated as different goddesses within the Norse myths, they share a number of staggeringly similar characteristics.

Frigg and Freyja have been linked due to their similarities: both Freyja and Frigg practice seid (see pages 103–109), both have a "falcon skin" that they use to fly, and both are associated with weaving and women's mysteries. Even their names sound similar.

There are a few differences between the two, however. Freyja is more closely associated with beauty, sexuality, and war than Frigg, while Frigg is more closely associated with weaving and wisdom, and is attended by a number of handmaidens. Frigg is also married to Odin (who's very well-known), while Freyja is married to Od (who's virtually unheard of).

The common explanation for why these two goddesses share such similar characteristics is that they were possibly, at one point in the ancient past, the same goddess. They may have split due to the development of different regional variations in pronouncing their names. The different deeds that were then attributed to the different names gave rise to two different goddesses.

However, Freyja and Frigg may still be reflections of each other in some ways, and perhaps the Norse accounted for this by bringing the two goddesses back together in the same stories.

Frigg's role in the Norse paradigm is that of the Allmother, and she's considered the only person wiser than Odin himself. She plays a very maternal role, perhaps representing the archetype of "mother" or "grandmother" within the Norse cosmology, being the oldest married woman of the family who stands at the head of the house.

Freyja, on the other hand, is more archetypical of young women. She's promiscuous, attentive to her appearance, and finds herself at the mercy of numerous awkward marriage proposals. She's associated with new relationships, newlyweds, and new mothers, suggesting that most of her qualities deal with the youthful stages of womanhood and the rites of passage that come with that.

Freyja and Frigg represent the archetypes of two different stages of life, as well as the kind of family members the Norse people would have experienced within their own society. Ultimately, all the gods represent the concepts of people and family, and thus fill those roles, Freyja and Frigg included.

Interestingly enough, we don't see Freyja and Frigg interacting with each other in the Norse myths very much. This may be intentional, or it may be due to some other reason, such as the nature of how they were divided as goddesses.

FREYJA AND JEWELRY

Jewelry has a strong connection with Freyja as both a decoration and a source of power. This is due to the fact that she owns a fantastic necklace known as the Brisingamen, which was forged by the dwarves.

JEWELRY IN NORSE CULTURE

The Norse loved their jewelry. Their most famous jewelry work took the form of the hammer pendants made for the god Thor. Less known, but still just as distinct, were the beads the Norse women wore across the front of their dresses. These were strung between two metal brooches that fastened the two straps of the dress, which they wore over a smock with longer sleeves. The strung beads were made of amber, bone, glass, or silver. Glass beads in particular were a favorite of the Norse people, and they could be either plain or decorative.

Women also wore pendants and bracelets: One such pendant from Viking times, made of silver, depicts Freyja herself. The Norse people, however, did not appear to wear any earrings.

ROCKS, MINERALS, AND METALS ASSOCIATED WITH FREYJA

Many modern practitioners associate Freyja with various gemstones and metals, which they use in crafts and jewelry dedicated to her. The stones and metals associated with Freyja include the following:

Amber: Naturally, Freyja is connected with amber as she is said to cry tears of red-gold, or amber. Amber is linked to healing.

Bronze: An alloy of copper and tin, bronze was used to make jewelry for a very long time.

Carnelian: Carnelian is a stone of strength, courage, and passion.

Citrine: Citrine is an energizing stone with sun-like properties.

Copper: Copper was, and still is, used in many jewelry pieces.

Emerald: A brilliant precious gemstone, emerald is a stone of love, partnerships, and friendships.

Fire agate: Fire agates are naturally brilliant and iridescent, containing that fire-like quality that Freyja loves so much. Fire agate is associated with passion and sex.

Gold: A yellow metal known for its luster and connection with sunlight. Freyja is also known as the lady of gold.

Green tourmaline: Green tourmaline promotes compassion and love.

Hawk eye: Hawk eye stones are associated with Freyja due to the fact that she transforms herself into a falcon to travel and survey the world.

Malachite: Malachite is a powerful stone that can be used for psychic intuition. However, it's quite toxic, so make sure only to handle it in its polished forms.

Moonstone: Moonstones are thought to increase psychic awareness. Good for seid.

Nordic gold: Nordic gold is a copper alloy used for coins in many European currencies. It has antimicrobial properties.

Rose quartz: This pink quartz is associated with love and passion.

Ruby: Ruby is a rich precious stone that is thought to encourage a passion for life.

Silver: Silver is a precious metal used in many jewelry pieces and is thought to be a powerful conduit for magic. An ancient amulet depicting Freyja was found to be made of silver.

Tourmaline: Tourmaline is a stone useful in shamanistic practices.

Vanadinite: An amber-colored stone that is useful for grounding. Take care as it is toxic.

FREYJA AND GULLVEIG

In previous pages we looked at Freyja's connection with Frigg. Here we will look at Freyja's link to Gullveig, a seeress in Norse mythology.

The poem *Völuspá*, or the Prophecy of the Seeress, is the first poem found within the *Poetic Edda*. The prophecy is recited to Odin, who wants to know the eventual fate of the gods, by an unnamed seeress who is sometimes thought to be Freyja in a trance channeling an older seeress. It begins with the seeress talking about all the events that came before until she reaches the present, then she talks about what she sees in the future.

In her recollections of the past, the seeress mentions a mysterious figure named Gullveig in connection to the Aesir–Vanir War. The story goes like this:

One day Gullveig arrives in Asgard, and the gods impale her with spears and burn her in Odin's hall. Three times she's burned, and three times she's reborn. On her third rebirth, she takes the name Heid (*Heiðr* in Old Norse, which means "shining one") and begins practicing seid, the magic of the wise.

The stanza in the Henry Adam Bellows translation of the *Poetic Edda* goes like this:

The war I remember, the first in the world,
When the gods with spears had smitten Gollveig,
And in the hall of Hor had burned her,
Three times burned, and three times born,
Oft and again, yet ever she lives.
Heith they named her who sought their home,
The wide-seeing witch, in magic wise;
Minds she bewitched that were moved by her magic,
To evil women a joy she was.

Some scholars think Gullveig/Heid is the same figure as Freyja. After all, it was Freyja who first taught Odin magic, while Snorri Sturluson's *Ynglinga Saga* depicts Freyja as the one who originally brought the art of seid to the Aesir.

However, that still leaves us with one question: What is this passage depicting? At first glance this looks like an act of violence, one that may have even triggered the Aesir–Vanir War. But it could also be describing a ritual death instead. These were not always represented in literal terms, but instead take on allegorical meanings. The Aesir piercing Gullveig with spears is very reminiscent of Odin's death on Yggdrasil, where he hung from the World Tree for nine days and nights pierced by a spear. We also see ritual burning in another poem, *Grímnismál*, which features a wanderer named Grimnir who was bound up and placed between two fires until he began to recite ecstatic poetry, revealing himself to be the Allfather, Odin.

Both of these apparent tortures represent initiation into the mysteries of the universe. Since the *Völuspá* recalls the history of the gods inasmuch as it foretells their fate, Gullveig's burning may represent the first creation of seid, which coincides with the first war ever fought.

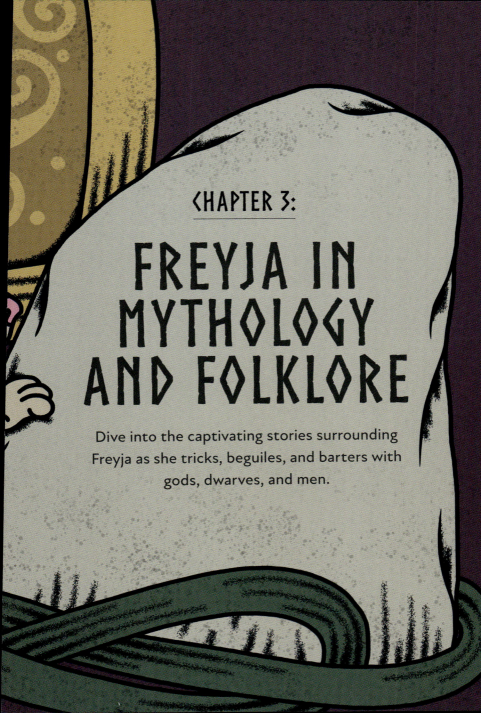

CHAPTER 3:
FREYJA IN MYTHOLOGY AND FOLKLORE

Dive into the captivating stories surrounding Freyja as she tricks, beguiles, and barters with gods, dwarves, and men.

A NOTE FOR THE READER

Often when we read, we read quietly to ourselves. But to gain a full experience of the Norse myths, we must experience them the same way the Norse people did hundreds of years ago...

In 1993, the German researcher Edward Wachtel published a paper recounting an astounding experience he had while interacting with prehistoric cave art in France. The first destination on Wachtel's journey was a cave system called Les Combarelles, in the Dordogne, which was well funded and brightly lit. But Wachtel had trouble understanding the cave art he was looking at because the pictures were drawn in a way that didn't make any sense: The animals were depicted in multiple poses, with each pose etched on top of another. This mystified Wachtel until he visited his next destination in the Dordgone, a cave called La Mouthe, which was poorly marked, poorly preserved, and lacked any sort of lighting. His tour guide was a local farmer, Monsieur Lapeyre, who, instead of a flashlight, used a gas-lit lantern to guide him in the cave.

It was under these dimly lit conditions that Edward Wachtel understood why the cave paintings looked the way they did—they were meant to be viewed by the flickering light of a fire. He encouraged Lapeyre to swing the lantern while standing a few feet away from the wall, and as the farmer did so, the animals on the cave walls began to move, their pigments growing brighter or darker and their poses shifting from one pose to the next depending on where the light and shadows fell. What Wachtel didn't understand when viewing the cave art in bright light, he understood by experiencing it in the conditions in which it was created; in the light of flickering fire. Wachtel saw another dimension of depth in the art that would have otherwise been absent.

Norse mythology works in a remarkably similar way, and faces a strikingly similar problem: For those of us removed from the Scandinavian oral tradition, our typical approach to the Norse myths is to read them silently to ourselves at any impersonal hour of the day. But this creates a similar effect to looking at cave paintings under bright lights—the change of medium causes us to lose an entire dimension of understanding.

In order to experience the full impact of the Norse myths, we need to replicate the conditions in which these stories were created. Fortunately, the way to do this is rather straightforward.

During the evening or at night, find time to settle down in front of a fire or some candles, or at least in an environment with a low-level light source, preferably incandescent in nature. Turn off any TVs or radios, and reduce any other considerable sources of noise. The goal is to tailor your environment to promote the sensation of "feeling cozy and content while sitting around the fire with loved ones"—a sensation known as *hygge* in modern-day Danish. The feeling of *hygge* is something that is shaped inside you by the visceral sensation of your environment. It's best not to try to "manifest" the feeling inside you based on the theoretical idea of it.

Once you've created this environment and are settled within it, the next step is to read the myths in this chapter out loud, slowly and quietly to yourself, the inner child. By "inner child," I don't mean your recollection of who you were as a child, but rather the child-mind that we all have inside us right now. This is that child's opportunity to once again experience the excitement and joy of being told a story.

It's alright if you can't do these things at this exact moment. The point of this passage is to give you the knowledge you need to experience the Norse myths when an opportunity does present itself.

It's also alright if you don't feel a sense of *hygge* right away, despite promoting it in your environment. This can happen if we lead particularly busy or stressful lives, and all it means is that our bodies need time to remember how to relax. We can encourage this by letting ourselves have the small creature comforts that bring us gladness and inner peace.

When you can, though, I encourage you to read the following myths out loud to yourself.

ROUND THE CAMPFIRE

Telling these myths around an outdoor campfire also works exceptionally well for this exercise. If you're in company, you or another member of the group may say these stories out loud. Remember to speak slowly and softly.

THE AESIR–VANIR WAR

In early times, the two tribes of gods, the Aesir and the Vanir, clashed in a terrible war. Freyja belonged to the Vanir and was traded as part of a hostage deal along with her brother Frey and her father Njord.

The first war in the world was known as the Aesir–Vanir War, and it was fought between two tribes of gods. One was called the Aesir, who were made up of Odin and his warriors, and the other was the Vanir, who were gods from a realm of green lands and bright skies.

Why the war broke out is lost to time, but the battle was fierce and bloody, and both sides fought mercilessly. After days of skirmishing, the war finally ended and the two families of gods met in the middle of the battlefield to forge a truce.

Oaths were sworn and contracts negotiated. When everything was completed, the Aesir and the Vanir brought forth hostages to exchange as a way of finalizing the agreements—they had promised each other only their finest.

Odin and the Aesir sent two men—one old and one younger—named Mimir and Hoenir. Mimir was a wise giant who owned a magic wellspring that granted great wisdom to those who drank from it. Hoenir was Odin's own brother, pleasing to look at and very well-built. The Vanir elected Hoenir as their chief at once.

The Vanir, meanwhile, sent over Njord and his two children, Frey and Freyja. Njord was a sea-loving god who kept his hall Noatun in the watery abodes where ships would sail. He could command the waves and grant calm seas and mild winds for those who asked. He was so dashing that the Aesir liked him immediately.

Frey was a beautiful young man who brought fertile grounds and mild rains to the land of Asgard. Flowers bloomed brightly and the grass became vibrant and green in his presence. He was later gifted a magical, cloud-like, foldable boat, which he could take across sea or sky, and a golden boar named Gullinbursti, whose bristles shone like sunbeams.

And lastly came Freyja. She radiated such beauty that everyone was immediately taken by her, but none dared to lay a finger on her for fear of her great skills as a warrior. She was also well versed in seid, a special kind of magic known only by women. With it, Freyja could manifest any outcome she desired.

Njord, Frey, and Freyja quickly proved themselves to be valuable and indispensable additions to the Aesir tribe, soon finding themselves at home among the Aesir gods.

Mimir and Hoenir, on the other hand, ran into trouble: Hoenir couldn't seem to make decisions as chief without Mimir telling him what to do, and the Vanir felt as if they had been cheated out of a fair swap—the Aesir had promised their best, but had only given their second best.

So, to express their great disapproval, the Vanir cut off Mimir's head and sent it back to Odin. This suited Odin just fine: He embalmed Mimir's head and used it as an oracle, consulting it for all kinds of advice thereafter.

FREYJA ESCAPES MARRIAGE

In this tale of how Asgard got its wall, a master mason wages that he can build a wall for the Aesir within one winter in exchange for the sun, the moon... and Freyja.

The Aesir gods had just finished establishing the mortal world of Midgard and were completing their work on the hall, Valhalla. But their new home lacked any fortification to protect them from the mountain- and frost-giants; the wilderness outside could invade their domicile without second thought.

Yet just as the gods were pondering this concerning dilemma, along came a man of *jötun*-stock, driving a cart pulled by an enormous black horse. As luck would have it, he was a mason, and upon seeing the Aesir's plight, he offered to build them a wall so robust that it would keep out all hostilities, even if they should come in through Midgard.

However, the mason would not accept gold or silver in exchange for such a difficult task. Instead, he required a very steep sum—he asked for the sun and the moon, *and* to have Freyja as his wife.

"Absolutely not!" scoffed Freyja when she heard of the deal. "I will not be traded away like some bargaining chip! And for a wall, no less!"

None of the other Aesir gods were too fond of this idea either. For one thing, they all wished to keep Freyja. For another, what would they do without the sun and moon?

So the Aesir hatched a scheme to enjoy the best of both worlds.

The gods returned to the mason and told him he could have what he wished, but only if he managed to build the wall in just one winter. If, on the first day of

EXCHANGING FREYJA

More than one story in the Norse myths features predicaments where dwarves and giants wish to wed or sleep with Freyja. This may be on account of Freyja's beauty, but it also speaks to something about Freyja's nature as a divine force. Her name, after all, means "lady," which suggests she represents the archetype of beauty and womanhood itself. Anyone who pines for a girlfriend or a wife, but hasn't fallen in love with a specific person yet, can be thought of as pining for Freyja—if not Freyja herself, then certainly all that she represents. This is generally what it means when any being in the Norse myths covets Freyja and aims to take her as a wife. But, of course, the myths also address the fact that Freyja's not interested in marrying those who don't know her as a person and are simply infatuated with her. It's only in later stories, crafted after the Viking Age, that we see anyone really get their way with her.

summer, anything was left unfinished, he would forfeit his payment. Additionally, he was to receive no help from any man with the work. He was to build the wall single-handedly—a feat that was difficult even for giants.

The mason scratched his chin, and said, "Alright, I'll do it on one condition: I ask that my horse, Svadilfari, assist me with the work."

Freyja and the gods were instantly uncertain, but it was Loki who swayed their minds. "Sure!" he said. "Why not? Where's the harm in entertaining a losing bet, anyway?"

The Aesir agreed that it didn't seem like much to ask; even with help loading and unloading the stone, the mason would still have to build the wall himself.

Many binding oaths and promises were then struck between the two parties, assuring the builder that he would be safe from Thor—who killed giants—so long as the contracts were observed.

Thor himself was not around to witness this agreement. He was off in a distant land fighting wild foes with his hammer Mjolnir. Satisfied that she was safe, Freyja returned to her hall.

The first day of winter rolled around and the mason got to work. By day he constructed the wall and by night he hauled up stone with Svadilfari.

What magnificent strength this stallion had, hauling cartful after cartful of enormous rocks! The horse also performed at twice the speed of the mason, so the wall quickly grew more complete with each passing day.

When summer was only three days away, it became clear that the mason would likely finish his difficult task. He had built a circular wall all the way around Asgard, and was close to meeting the end at the entrance.

Freyja grew apprehensive. A dispute broke out among the Aesir as they saw the wall gradually encircle their settlement. How had this happened? Who in their right mind had agreed to let Freyja be married off to a mason from Jötunheim? And who had consented to spoiling the sky with the removal of the sun and moon?

"It was Loki who persuaded us to grant the mason help from the horse!" Freyja said, standing up in fury. "He would never have been so close to finishing the wall had it not been for that horse!"

And with that, the Aesir all ganged up on Loki, who, suddenly fearing for his life, swore that he would fix the problem and make things right, doing whatever it took to achieve this.

That evening, as the mason drove Svadilfari through the woods to the quarry to collect stone, a sleek and beautiful mare came darting out in front of them, neighing at the mason's horse, kicking her hooves and tossing her head, before cantering back into the woods. Upon seeing how beautiful the horse was, the stallion tore off his bridle and chased wildly after the mare. The mason ran after them but could not keep up.

All through the night the stallion pursued the mare and the mason tracked the horses, so no work was done that night. The next day, the mason didn't build as much of the wall as before, and it became clear that the work was now too far behind for him to finish in time.

When the mason realized this, he flew into a violent rage. Fearing for their wellbeing, the Aesir cast aside their oaths and called upon Thor, who appeared the instant his name was evoked.

Thor raised his hammer skyward and brought it down on the mason's head, sending him straight to Helheim.

Freyja breathed a sigh of relief; she and the sun and moon would not be given away after all.

The Aesir finished the last of the wall, and for a while there was peace. Nine months later, Loki returned. With him was a mottled gray colt with eight legs. This horse, which he had borne as a mare with Svadilfari, was named Sleipnir. Loki gave Sleipnir to Odin as a gift, and the little gray colt grew to become the swiftest of all horses.

BREAKING OATHS

In a time before societies developed robust legal systems, the Norse relied on social agreements and taboos to uphold contracts. They used stories to impart to listeners why being fair and honest was important when making oaths or doing business with anyone, by demonstrating what happens when we don't. Many of the Norse myths show the Aesir breaking the oaths they make with others through dishonesty and trickery, causing other beings to become resentful of the gods. Eventually, this behavior creates a disastrous future for them, known as Ragnarok. The Norse people themselves took oaths and honesty very seriously, perhaps because they were raised with a clear picture of what would happen if they didn't.

THE FORGING OF BRISINGAMEN

The story of Freyja's necklace appears in the *Flateyjarbók* (a medieval Icelandic manuscript) in a tale called *Sörla þáttr*, penned long after the Viking Age. This Christianized medieval tale depicts the Norse gods as humans in Asia, and Freyja as King Odin's concubine.

Freyja's necklace was a treasure known far and wide. It shone with the gold of the setting sun, glimmering with honey-like, amber tones that reflected light as bright as flames. When Freyja wore the necklace, it lit up her face with a warm glow, earning it the name Brisingamen, or the "necklace of fiery light." It was not long after she'd joined the Aesir that Freyja acquired this beautiful necklace.

One day, Freyja was out for a walk when she came across a hill that was open, very much like the ones inhabited by hidden folk such as trolls and dwarves. She crept closer, and what did she find on looking into the entrance but four dwarves at work in their smithy, hammering fine metals with their instruments and passing precious gems and ores to each other.

Sitting upon one of the dwarves' tables was the most beautiful and exquisite necklace that Freyja had ever seen.

The dwarves noticed Freyja looming in the entrance to the hill and were so struck by her beauty that they stopped their work just to stare at this new face.

"Who goes there?" asked the first dwarf, named Alfrigg.

"I have never seen you around these parts before," said the second dwarf, who was called Dvalin.

"You're not of the Aesir, are you?" said the third dwarf, Berling.

The fourth dwarf, whose name was Grerr, was silent, but he bobbed his head thoughtfully.

"I'm Freyja of the Aesir," the goddess replied. "I come from Vanaheim like my father Njord and my brother Frey. But more importantly..." —and here she pointed to the necklace— "... how much are you selling that for? If you want gold, I have gold. If you want silver, I have silver. And if you want something other than those, just name your price."

Freyja smiled at the dwarves with a light in her eyes. The necklace would be hers, no matter what the price.

The four dwarves exchanged glances with each other before drawing close into a huddle, whispering among themselves. Freyja waited, and soon the four of them broke their circle and looked at her once more.

"We ask not for gold or silver or other such things," Alfrigg said. "But rather that each of us spends one night in your arms. For that price alone, you may have the beautiful necklace."

This was a price Freyja was willing to pay. She agreed and slept with one of the dwarves each night for four consecutive nights. On the morning of the fifth day, she walked away from the hill with her new necklace glimmering around her neck, pleased with her "purchase."

THE THEFT OF FREYJA'S NECKLACE

Freyja's necklace is stolen soon after she "buys" it from the dwarves, with Loki getting involved in the caper. Originally characterizing Freyja as the concubine of Odin, the Allfather catches wind of her escapades and is displeased. He sends Loki to steal her necklace, so he can blackmail her into "earning" it back.

Out of all the Aesir, no god seemed to know quite as much gossip as Loki. Whenever there were any rumors floating about, Loki frequently caught wind of them, no matter how covertly they were spread.

It came to pass one day that Loki had his ear close to the ground and heard murmuring among the dwarves below. They were chattering about how Freyja had obtained her new necklace—that she had not paid for it with gold or silver, but instead by the wealth of her thighs.

Later that evening, when Loki was visiting Valhalla, he let slip to Odin the rumors he had heard. The Allfather frowned and said to him, "Fetch that necklace and bring it to me."

Odin knew Freyja lusted after jewelry but to sleep with four dwarves... surely this must have been a spectacular necklace indeed.

Loki shook his head. "There's slim chance of that," he said. "The doors to Freyja's retreat are impossible to enter when locked."

"Then see to it that you find a way to get them open," Odin replied. "And don't come back until you do!"

So, Loki left Valhalla swearing and cursing to himself, wishing he hadn't opened his mouth about the necklace.

Loki wandered up to Freyja's personal retreat in Asgard—a stout wooden house with doors made of slats of wood so perfectly aligned there was hardly a crack to be seen between them. He grabbed the handles of the doors to her retreat and tried to open them, but they were bolted fast from the inside. He turned his back to the doors and slumped down, feeling deflated.

Soon it began to get darker and colder, and Loki shivered as the wind whipped between the buildings around him.

But Loki's clever mind was at work, and, as the sun began to rise, he transformed into the shape of a fly, scouring all the wooden slats in the doors to find an entry point. The retreat was so well-built that he could only find a space the size of an iron nail between one of the joints. After much effort he managed to squeeze his fly-body through the gap.

Loki found Freyja fast asleep in her bed, with the necklace shining around her neck. In the next moment, Loki transformed himself into a little flea, sat on her cheek, and bit her. Freyja cursed and swatted Loki away before turning over—revealing the clasp of the necklace. Very soon she fell asleep again.

Loki cast aside the flea-form for his usual one, and with nimble fingers he quickly undid the necklace clasp. Chuckling to himself, he quietly unbolted the door of the dwelling and snuck out, leaving the door open a crack behind him.

When Freyja awoke, she immediately knew something was wrong. Raising her hand to her chest, she realized that her necklace was missing. She felt the chill morning air on her arms, and saw that the door was open. She cursed Loki's name, knowing that only he had the nerve to commit such a slippery theft.

Donning her armor and cloak, Freyja also knew that no one other than Odin would have commanded him to steal the necklace. She marched straight to Valhalla, where she found Odin waiting for her, necklace in hand.

"Odin, you've done a fiendish thing, sending your right-hand man to rob me!" Freyja cried. "Give me back Brisingamen at once!"

But Odin shook his head, turning the necklace this way and that, admiring the glint of light upon the jewels.

"You won't get it back at this rate, considering how you've come by it," he said sourly.

Freyja wondered if he was jealous of the dwarves. She considered offering a kind of reconciliation, but decided that she was too angry to even try. "Well then, what do you want?" she asked.

Without pausing, Odin said, "There are two kingdoms in Midgard. I want you to use your magic to make them fight each other for all eternity."

This was an odd request, but it wasn't too out of character for Odin, and as they were both war-deities, Freyja was sure she could make it happen the way he wanted, especially if it meant getting back her necklace.

Whatever the reason Odin wanted the two kingdoms to fight is between him and Freyja alone. Either way, she succeeded, and Odin returned her beautiful necklace.

HEIMDALL RETURNS FREYJA'S NECKLACE

In another story, Loki steals Freyja's necklace again, but this time, his motive is unknown. Perhaps he was bored and wanted to entertain himself, or perhaps he had more nefarious plans in mind. However, in this version of the story, he is caught red-handed by Heimdall, Odin's son, and the watchman of Asgard. Loki attempts to flee by transforming into a seal and jumping into a river, only for Heimdall also to turn into a seal and follow him. Eventually, Heimdall steals the necklace back from Loki and returns it to Freyja. The return of the necklace was depicted in paintings by various artists for an 1846 competition organized by the Royal Swedish Academy of Fine Arts, all of which show just how relieved Freyja is to have her necklace returned.

FREYJA'S LIFE IN ASGARD

Freyja entertains her own host of the dead, just as Odin does in his hall, Valhalla.

When Freyja first arrived in Asgard from Vanaheim, she rode on a chariot pulled by two large and magnificent cats, with long ears and dense coats.

In Freyja's lap were her daughters, Hnoss and Gersemi, both of whom brought delight to all.

Freyja's husband, Od, was missing, however. He was a wanderer by nature and always meandering from realm to realm. On occasion Freyja would don a disguise and walk among mortals, going by names such as Mardoll, Horn, Syr, and Gef, in search of her husband.

FREYJA AND SUNLIGHT

Many depictions of Freyja connect her and her brother Frey with sunlight. The imagery around Freyja is often gleaming or brilliant in nature; her necklace shines with an amber luster, and she sheds sparkling red-gold tears. Considering Freyja's father is Njord, a sea-god, she may be linked to the way sunlight sparkles and glimmers on ocean waves, the same way her brother is linked to beams of light shining through the clouds.

As she traveled, she would cry, and her tears would be brilliant red-gold. Some believe these tears became amber and would fill the Baltic Sea.

When Freyja was not searching for her husband, she was either back home in Asgard or on the battlefield. Whenever there was a fight, Freyja would put on her armor and ride into the fray with her valkyries. Galloping across the sky, they would scoop up the warriors who had fallen in battle and carry them off to the heavens.

Such was Freyja's prowess in battle that it impressed Odin, and so he allowed her the first pick of half the warriors who fell in battle. So, while some of the fallen went to Odin, where they would enjoy feasting and skirmishing in his hall Valhalla, the rest went to Freyja and her abode, Folkvang, sometimes described as a hall and other times as a shimmering field. Within Folkvang was Freyja's hall, Sessrumnir, a large and magnificent place with room for all. Here, warriors could find rest and respite after fighting difficult battles.

THE THEFT OF THOR'S HAMMER

A tale in which Thor wakes up to find his hammer Mjolnir has gone missing. Loki discovers that it has been stolen by the giant Thrym, who will only return it if the Aesir give him Freyja as his bride. While the Aesir do send him a "bride," it is not Freyja...

One day Freyja awoke to the sound of someone pounding at her door. Pulling on her cloak, she walked to the doors of her hall and opened them. Thor rolled in without so much as a greeting or a look, his brow furrowed and his beard bristling. Behind him trailed Loki, whose face looked pale and fraught.

Bewildered and suspicious of the duo, Freyja left her doors open and crossed her arms, sighing.

"What happened now?" she asked, for Thor and Loki only came to her like this when something bad had happened.

Finally, Thor turned to her. "Freyja," he grumbled, "my hammer has been stolen, and we need help finding it."

"I have offered to search for Thor's hammer," said Loki. "But I'll need to travel far and wide to places unreachable in order to find it." He rubbed his hands together and shot a swift glance at Freyja. "Will you lend us your cloak of feathers, Freyja?"

Freyja nodded without hesitation. Her feathered cloak allowed the wearer to transform into the shape of a falcon, which could be used to travel to countries far beyond Asgard.

"I'd lend it to you even if it were made of silver!" she said. "I'd lend it to you even if it were made of gold!" She undid the clasp of the feathered cloak she wore and handed it over to Loki. She watched as he donned the cloak and saw his shape change into that of a falcon. Quickly, Loki flapped his wings and took off out of one of Freyja's windows, and she bit her lip as she watched him disappear from sight.

As Loki searched, Freyja waited in her hall with her warriors. Thor, in the meantime, wandered throughout Asgard. Both of them were set on keeping the hammer's disappearance a secret, so as to not cause a panic among the Aesir. Freyja didn't always like Loki meddling with her business, and she certainly didn't like it when he involved her with his schemes, but he had never used her feathered

cloak irresponsibly, and this time seemed more pertinent than ever that he use it.

Eventually, her wandering thoughts took her feet to wander outside, where she saw Thor looking up at the sky. Gazing upward as well, she spotted Loki in falcon-form flying toward Asgard.

Thor shouted up at Loki, halting him in his flight. "Have you had any luck in your travels? Tell me what you found while still airborne, for a man who's sitting is prone to forgetting his tales, while the reclining man divulges nothing but lies!"

So, Loki, circling above, said from the air: "My efforts have not been in vain! I traveled to Jötunheim, the land of the giants, and Thrym, the king of giants, has your hammer. He says that no man will ever be able to take it back, unless they bring him Freyja to be his wife!"

Freyja was so shocked by this that she immediately turned away from the pair and headed straight back to her hall. Of all the nerve, being sought after in exchange for Thor's hammer! No sooner had she closed the doors behind her that Thor stormed in with Loki at his heels.

"Tie on a bridal headdress, Freyja!" he boomed. "The king of the giants, Thrym, has my hammer, and he will give it back to me in exchange for taking you as his wife! The two of us shall go to Jötunheim!"

Freyja turned a venomous expression upon Thor. "No, no, and a thousand times no!" she cried. "Not for walls, not for hammers, not for anything!"

Freyja stormed about so much that her spectacular necklace, the Brisingamen, snapped from around her neck. "I would look all too eager journeying with you to Jötunheim, Thor!"

She saw Thor pout and his face grow as red as his beard. He pulled at his beard and grumbled in anger, but Freyja knew this was just a tantrum as well as anyone.

"The fact is, we still need to get Mjolnir back," Loki mentioned as he handed Freyja her falcon cloak.

"Then I suppose we'll have to break the news about it," she said, donning it. She picked up Brisingamen and returned it to her neck.

When the news broke about Thor's missing hammer, the Aesir held a council and debated what could be done to get it back.

"Are you sure we can't just marry off Freyja?" they mumbled to themselves. But Freyja slammed her hands upon the table.

"As if any of you would like to be married off to some random giant-king in the mountains!" she protested.

"Now hold on, there's something to that," the watchman of the Aesir, Heimdall, said. "If Freyja won't go with Thor to giant-country, then let's have Thor wear Brisingamen and go as the bride himself!" The other gods laughed at this suggestion as Freyja's hand shot to the prized necklace around her throat. "Let keys hang by his side, let the wedding dress fall below his knees, and let the bridal jewels hang across his breast! We shall put the pointed headdress on his head instead!"

Thor stomped with fury. "And let everyone in Asgard view me as perverse for it!" he cried. "Absolutely not!"

"Now, come on Thor, don't say that!" said Loki encouragingly. "We'll have giants besieging Asgard if we don't get your hammer back soon!"

After much hemming and hawing, Thor agreed. He let the keys hang by his side, the wedding dress fall below his knees, and the bridal jewels hang across his breast. Freyja reluctantly allowed them to borrow her necklace, as this was a better option than marrying the giant herself.

The Aesir hung Brisingamen around Thor's neck and put the pointed headdress on his head, allowing the veil to hide his face.

Then Loki appeared, disguised as a handmaiden, and said, "I will go with you as the bride's handmaiden! Now off we go to Jötunheim!"

And so Thor's goats were harnessed to his chariot and they galloped quickly to giant-country. Mountains split and lightning flashed as they went.

From Jötunheim, Thrym saw the unmistakable approach of Thor's chariot.

"Look alive, my fellow giants, and spread straw upon the hall benches!" he cried. "The Aesir are bringing Freyja to be my wife, Njord's daughter from Noatun! Many riches I have in life—gold-horned cows walking in my yards and jet-black oxen in all their splendour! I have troves of treasures and heaps of luxuries! But what I don't have is the beautiful Freyja. Only she seems to be missing from all my many treasures."

The chariot arrived early that evening, and the wedding banquet was served. Thrym watched as the bride downed one whole ox, eight salmon, all the little delicacies made for the women, and three caskets of mead.

"I've never seen a bride with such a hearty appetite!" said Thrym.

The bride's clever-looking handmaiden sat before him, and said: "Why, it's because Freyja ate nothing for eight days, so eager was she to come to Jötunheim!"

At this Thrym was overjoyed and eager to kiss his wife-to-be, but no sooner had he bent under the bridal veil than he staggered back across the hall.

"Freyja, my love, why are your eyes so fierce?" he cried. "It is as though a fire burns within them!"

And at this, the bride's clever-looking handmaiden said: "That's because Freyja did not sleep for eight nights, so madly in love is she with you!"

"Ah, so that is the truth then, my love?" said Thrym. "But why does she not speak to me herself?"

And at this, the bride's clever-looking handmaiden said: "Why, it's because Freyja has not spoken a single word for eight days and nights, so enamored is she with you!"

And upon hearing this, Thrym could wait no longer. "That's it!" he cried. "Bring out the hammer and let's consecrate the bride!"

And so Thor's hammer was brought out and set upon his lap. Thor's heart laughed in his breast and his courage soared as he grasped the hammer and raised it above his head. He quickly did away with Thrym and smashed the heads of the rest of his court as well.

Thor and Loki made their escape, the chariot blazing and thunder and lighting booming and crashing all around.

And in this way, Thor got his hammer back, while Freyja remained at home, peacefully unwed to anyone except her dear absent Od.

FREYJA RIDES WITH HYNDLA

A relatively late edition to the *Poetic Edda*, the *Lay of Hyndla* is a story in which Freyja discovers the ancestry of her faithful servant, Ottar, by prying the information out of a giantess named Hyndla.

There was once a man named Ottar who was utterly devoted to Freyja. So great was his love for the goddess that he made her a stone shrine and altar, upon which he left many offerings and libations. Freyja returned his adoration in kind, and the two became lovers.

One day, however, Ottar was in a dismal mood. He sat at the stone altar and sighed.

"What's wrong, dear Ottar?" Freyja asked him.

"I'm in an terrible state," Ottar replied. "I've wagered a bet with a man named Angantyr. In three days' time, we shall have a boasting contest to find out whose family is more noble. But there's just one problem: My lineage has been kept from me. I don't know who my father is nor who my mother is or any who came before. If I only knew my ancestry, I could claim the gold we have bet on and make a name for myself."

"You've shown me nothing but love and devotion," said Freyja, "I shall see to it that these things are revealed. I know of a giantess named Hyndla who is familiar with all family lines, even those that no man knows or remembers. But she guards these secrets closely and will not give up her knowledge easily: We will have to trick them out of her."

And so Freyja instructed Ottar to brew a special elixir so he could travel down the way of the slain—the roads the dead walk to reach Valhalla. It is on these roads that the mysteries are stored, including knowledge that has been lost to time.

"And now for our deception," announced Freyja.

And with that, Freyja transformed her lover into a giant boar with golden bristles, similar to her brother Frey's. She threw herself upon the boar's back and took off down the roads of the dead.

Soon Freyja reached Hyndla's cave, and she called out to the giantess:

"Maiden, sister, my friend, awaken!
Stir from your hollow cave and walk with me!
The darkness falls fast and I must ride to Valhalla.
I must ride on to seek the great hall!
That is my mission here; to see the Allfather,
Who has granted many boons to many men:
Triumph for some and treasure to others,
Wisdom to poets and courage to warriors.
Come forth and lead with your wolf,
That beast who embodies the ferocity of your thoughts.
Your steed runs faster than my own noble boar,
Who I do not wish to coax into a run."

Hyndla emerged from the cave, riding on top of her wolf; a familiar that embodied the speed of her thoughts

and the strength of her ability to recall information. But the giantess eyed Freyja with suspicion, and said:

*I sense deception in your words, Freyja.
One look at your steed tells me enough;
Those aren't the eyes of just any boar,
But those of your lover, Ottar, the son of Instein.*

The boar's ears pricked up on hearing the name of his father, Instein, a champion of King Half of Horthaland, in Norway. But Freyja patted the boar's golden body, and said:

*I think you must be dreaming to suspect
That my lover is with me on the roads of the slain;
You are correct in saying the boar is not my thoughts.
It is the beast named Gullinbursti, crafted by the dwarves.
But let us make haste and talk now of my lover.
For I fear he seeks his lineage, and he will find a bloody fate.
Tell me his heritage at length, Hyndla,
So I can be sure that he never stumbles upon it.*

Hyndla nodded, and the two of them took their steeds down the roads of the slain. Hyndla raced ahead as Freyja kept pace from behind. Said Hyndla:

*His name is Ottar, the son of Instein,
Who is the son of Alf the Old,
Alf was the son of Ulf, and Ulf the son of Sefari,
And Sefari's father was Svan the Red.
Ottar's mother is the priestess Hledis;
Frothi is her father and Friaut her mother;
She is bright with bracelets fair
And of the mightiest of mankind.*

As the giantess spoke, images of people and ghosts blurred passed them. There was Ottar's father, a champion, and his mother, a great priestess. On and on Hyndla went, recalling heroes and kings of old, each of them blurring past. Ottar was mesmerized by the people he saw as the giantess spoke.

Finally, Hyndla retraced his ancestry all the way back to the gods and goddesses themselves. By the time Hyndla had finished, they'd raced to the end of the road, reaching Valhalla.

Freyja dismounted from the boar's back. "And now, Hyndla," she said, "give my boar your dram of enchanted memory-beer, so that he may remember everything that was said for the next three days."

The giantess scowled. "What for?" she asked suspiciously.

"So that he can recall his lineage on the day he spars with Angantyr," Freyja replied, smiling.

"So the boar is Ottar after all!" the giantess spat. "You've deceived me! I refuse to do you the favor, Freyja!"

But at this Freyja simply raised her hands with intent and began to utter an enchantment:

*"Around the giantess flames shall rise,
So you may not ride from this place unburned."*

Hyndla felt herself quickly grow hot, and she shouted out at the sudden pain. "Fine! Have it your way!" she said.

Hyndla pulled a dram of liquid from her satchel and passed it to Freyja. "I warn you," she said. "No good comes from giving humanity secrets that they haven't won themselves. I've seen in my visions a warning of what this brings, and it's the same as that which was

foretold to the Allfather by the seeress of old—Ragnarok, the fate of the gods. I saw an ax-age, a wind-age, a wolf-age. I saw brother fighting brother, shields splintering to pieces, and the world crumbling to ash and darkness. This kind of deed brings that reality closer, Freyja. If you give this memory-beer to Ottar, he shall find that it's a cup poisoned with an evil destiny."

But Freyja scoffed. "I believe I know threats when I see them," she said. "I think Ottar will find this brew to be a fair and fine drink. And besides, I love my beloved Ottar, and now he will become a rich and powerful man. What harm can possibly come of it?"

Freyja took the dram from Hyndla and gave it to Ottar. And, just as she had hoped, he won the wager and became wealthy and famous from his ill-got gold.

RAGNORAK

Ragnarok, which means "the destiny of the gods," is an event prophesied by a seeress, who may have been Freyja herself channeling the words and memories of a much older *völva*. Ragnarok is built on a network of consequences orchestrated by the Aesir's actions, and hinge around the events brought about by Loki's three children: Hel, a death-goddess who is a living girl on one side and a corpse on the other; Jormungand, a giant serpent who circles Midgard; and Fenrir, a huge, prideful wolf. Odin's treatment of these three, along with other disastrous consequences, culminates into the demise of the gods. The few that survive rebuild society.

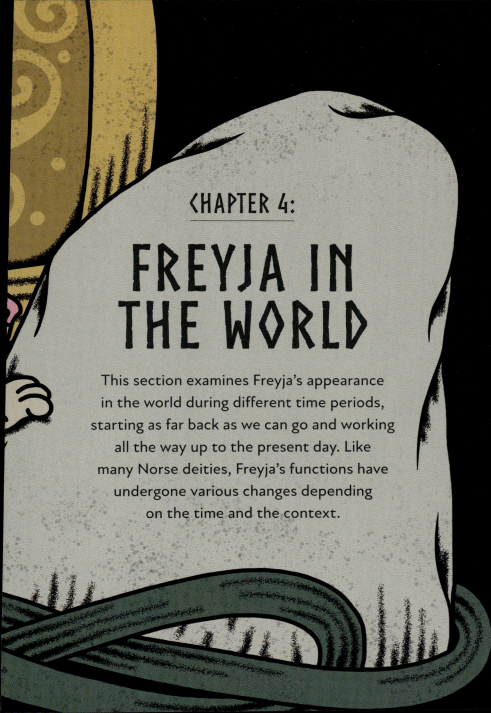

CHAPTER 4:
FREYJA IN THE WORLD

This section examines Freyja's appearance in the world during different time periods, starting as far back as we can go and working all the way up to the present day. Like many Norse deities, Freyja's functions have undergone various changes depending on the time and the context.

FREYJA BEFORE AND DURING THE VIKING AGE

Norse society rose up sometime after 500 BCE, correlating with the proto-Norse Bronze Age cultures moving into the Iron Age. The worship of Freyja as a goddess was likely established around this time, if not earlier.

Freyja and the goddess Frigg might have been one and the same early within the history of the Norse people. Why did a separation occur? The folklorist Ebbe Shön posits that it may be due to the rise of regional variations in how their original names were pronounced, leading to different deeds and features attributed to one name or the other (see *Freyja and Frigg*, page 51). As time passed, people eventually recognized them as different figures. A similar division may have happened between Frigg's husband, Odin, and Freyja's husband, Od.

However, it's unclear when Freyja and Frigg's separation occurred, and we may never be able to tell for certain. But there might be some clues. One of the oldest texts we have that records information about the Norse gods, *Germania*, was written in 98 BCE by a Roman politician named Tacitus. Within it, he mentions that the Germanic peoples worshipped four main deities: Mercury, Hercules, Mars, and Isis.

As was typical for Roman writers, Tacitus replaced the names of the Norse gods with deities the Romans would have been familiar with, swapping them out based on their similar attributes. We know Mercury, Hercules, and Mars correlate to Odin, Thor, and Tyr based on their attributes, but it's inconclusive who Isis is supposed to be. It's possible she might represent Frigg or Freyja due to her association with magic, but she might also represent the synthesis of both, and that this was during the time when Frigg and Freyja were one and the same.

FREYJA'S NAME IN THE WORLD

Freyja's long-term existence in the world is reflected in place names, or toponyms. We can see strong evidence of Freyja's worship by looking at locations in Scandinavia named after her. Some examples include Frölunda (Frö's Grove) in Sweden and Frøihov (Frö's Hof) in Norway. These places were named after Freyja to show she had a strong cult of worship there.

ARCHAEOLOGICAL FINDS

Archaeological evidence of Freyja points to a strong cult of worship before and during the Viking Age. As the goddess of magic, Freyja was intimately connected with the practices of *völva*, or wise women, and iconography associated with Freyja has been found in a number of *völva* graves, including items such as jewelry depicting her visage and necklaces reminiscent of Brisingamen.

A famous longship, mostly made of oak, known as the Oseberg ship, was discovered in a large burial mound in

Norway in 1903. Thought to be from the 9th century, it is one of the most crucial discoveries from the Viking Age. Excavations revealed a wagon or sledge, among other items, with a number of cats carved on the back of it, perhaps referencing Freyja's chariot. A distaff was also found, a tool associated with women and Freyja. It was likely purpose-built for a high-status burial, not only because the oars looked unused, but because the remains of two women were found, challenging notions that it would only be men who received such burials, and bringing women in the Viking Age into a new light for historians.

FREYJA IN MEDIEVAL TIMES

Most history books mark the end of the Viking Age with the Battle of Stamford Bridge, which took place in 1066 CE between the English army and Norwegian invaders. It gets the name from a single unidentified bridge that served as a bottleneck for the English army, and a single unnamed Viking who mounted a defense on the bridge. This Viking warrior cut down as many as 40 English soldiers before meeting his own demise, after which the Norwegians were slaughtered. (The Normans then defeated this English army three weeks later.)

While the end of the Viking Age wasn't triggered by this event, the Battle of Stamford Bridge allegorically marks the decline of Viking activities and the closure of Norse civilization. Through a combination of Christianization, political changes, shifting borders, and simply moving around a great deal, the Norse people's society was so transformed that it had become something other than Norse by that point.

Yet every Scandinavian I've spoken to refers to the Norse people as their ancestors and the Viking Age as their immediate history. The fact it's a pagan history doesn't diminish its importance.

This history was even acknowledged by medieval Icelandic writers, who, despite being Christian, took it upon themselves to write down the cultural stories (mythology) of Freyja and the rest of the Norse gods. These are mostly found in the *Poetic* and *Prose Eddas*. The existence of these texts and others preserves stories and important information about Freyja.

Though medieval texts provide some of the best documentation about the Norse gods, we can't always take them at face value. What we can trust about them depends on the author's intention, and, unfortunately, this did not always pertain to unbiased cultural preservation.

Fortunately, the *Prose* and *Poetic Eddas* seemed intent on preserving the pre-Christian stories about the Norse gods, even if they didn't necessarily preserve pre-Christian attitudes. So while we can't consider these books "scripture" by any means, we can still treat them as culturally significant.

FREYJA IN THE POETIC EDDA

As a main goddess of the Norse pantheon, Freyja appears in many places in the *Poetic Edda*. She's mentioned in the opening poem *Völuspá*, which is a prophecy given to Odin by an unknown seeress about the fate of the gods, referred to as Ragnarok. Some people speculate that this seeress might have been Freyja herself, or perhaps someone Freyja was channeling.

Freyja also plays a major role in the poem *Þrymskviða*, in which a giant called Thrym steals Thor's hammer (see *The Theft of Thor's Hammer*, pages 72–75).

Loki causes trouble for Freyja in the poem *Lokasenna*, where he accuses her of lustful deeds during a feast at the giant Aegir's hall. While Freyja herself is already known to be a loose woman, Loki spilling

the tea like this in public causes quite the scandal.

Freyja is the main character in the poem *Hyndluljóð*, in which she tricks the giantess Hyndla into revealing the ancestry of her lover, Ottar (see *Freyja Rides with Hyndla*, pages 76–79).

Freyja is also mentioned in passing in the poems *Oddrúnargrátr* and *Grímnismál*, but only briefly.

FREYJA IN THE PROSE EDDA

Snorri's *Prose Edda* talks about Freyja at some length. In the first book, known as *Gylfaginning* (or "The Tricking of King Gylfi"), Freyja is counted among the female goddesses (the Asynjur), and is referred to as the second-highest in rank after Frigg. It's also here that we are given descriptions of Freyja's halls and her activities of riding into battle. The *Prose Edda* also describes Freyja as approachable when she is prayed to and fond of love songs, and recommends praying to her for anything that concerns love and romance.

Freyja plays a large role in the story of the building of Asgard's wall (see *Freyja Escapes Marriage*, pages 62–65).

The next book in the *Prose Edda*, *Skáldskaparmál*, tells of another instance in which Freyja lends her feathered cloak to Loki, but this time to retrieve the goddess Idunn from Jötunheim, where she is held captive after being kidnapped.

The *Prose Edda* also alludes to another mysterious myth now lost to time in relation to Freyja. Heimdall is mentioned as being "the recoverer of Freyja's necklace," and this suggests that there was a tale in which Loki stole Freyja's necklace and Heimdall got it back.

Later, a passage describing gold refers to Freyja's connection with the precious metal, saying that gold may be referred to as Freyja's tears. Apparently, there was not much distinction between amber and gold in this sense.

FREYJA IN OTHER SAGAS

Freyja is mentioned in passing in a few other sagas too:

Sörla þáttr

This is a short narrative from a longer story found in the Icelandic *Flateyjarbók*, which recounts the tale of the forging of Brisingamen. In it, the gods are euhemerized (depicted as human beings), with Freyja cast as Odin's concubine. When she sees the brilliant Brisingamen, she agrees as payment to sleep with the four dwarves who crafted it (see *The Forging of Brisingamen*, page 67).

Hálfs Saga Ok Hálfsrekka

This legendary saga was written in the 14th century. In it, a king named Alrek has two wives, Signy and Geirhild, but he can't keep them both. So he tasks them to each brew ale for him before he returns home in the summer, and whoever brews the better ale will be kept. Signy prays to Freyja, while Geirhild prays to a man named Hott, who's really Odin in disguise. Odin spits in Geirhild's brew and ruins it, so it is Signy who wins the contest.

Egils Saga

Egils saga is a medieval Icelandic saga, the oldest manuscript of which dates back to 1250 CE. The saga recounts the deeds of Egil Skallagrímsson and his descendants. At one point during the saga, Skallagrímsson refuses to eat, and so too does his daughter. She states she will have no meal until she is joined together with Freyja in her hall.

Njáls Saga

Freyja is mentioned in a disparaging way in *Njáls saga*, a masterful work that was written in the 13th century. In it, the character Hjallti Skeggi sings a song that refers to both Freyja and Odin as dogs.

FREYJA IN MEDIEVAL FOLKLORE

As is the case sometimes with older mythology, not all the Norse deities have been recorded equally. Gods such as Thor and Odin are better attested to since their attributes were of greater concern for medieval writers. As a result, much of the women's oral traditions weren't preserved, including evidence of how Freyja was viewed and venerated.

However, the functions of these goddesses are implied in how Christian figures, such as the Virgin Mary, became relevant in medieval Scandinavian lives. These figures more or less assumed the roles previously fulfilled by pagan gods. Freyja (as well as Frigg) was once called upon for all matters pertaining to childbirth, but during the Middle Ages this role was taken over by the Virgin Mary instead. We can see this change reflected in a number of Scandinavian folk names for various plants and grasses associated with childbirth (see pages 38–39) which were eventually linked to the Virgin Mary instead.

Despite the demonization of the Norse gods during Scandinavia's medieval period, some positive depictions of Freyja persisted. The Swedish author Johan Alfred Göth wrote of a folk-belief relating to Freyja, thunderstorms, and the grain harvests: When children were afraid of thunder and lightning, their parents would tell them that it was Freyja hitting the ground with flint and steel to see if the grain was ripe, and that she was doing this to be helpful, unlike Thor, who would strike sheep and people just because he felt like it.

Other surviving folklore surrounding Freyja is connected with Yuletide customs. During pagan times, people would toast the Norse gods during Yule to ensure good growth and peace, with libations offered to Odin and to Frigg or Freyja. But King Hakon the Good supposedly issued a decree that these libations must be dedicated to Jesus and Mary instead, and thus the tribute was swapped.

A folk-belief in Värlend, Sweden, had it that Freyja came every Christmas night to shake the apple trees for a good harvest, and so people would leave apples for her as repayment. However, one needed to take care not to leave a plow outside on Christmas night because if Freyja sat on it, it would no longer be of any use.

Though perhaps not appearing as often in Scandinavian folk magic today as the Virgin Mary, Freyja was still evoked for Icelandic magical staves, or *galdrastafir*, recorded in grimoires—books of spells—from the 13th century.

A certain folklore that has endured since pre-Christian times is linked to the constellation of Orion, which in Swedish is known as *Friggerocken* or *Frejarocken* ("Frigg's distaff" or "Freyja's distaff"). For the Norse, this constellation may have looked like the figure of a woman weaving in the sky.

FREYJA'S EARLY MODERN-DAY REPRESENTATIONS

The Norse gods existed in obscurity within the rural countryside of Scandinavia until around the 1890s, when they were reintroduced to the world due to a growing interest in the pre-Christian past among Europeans. This was especially true within Germany, during a period characterized by German Romanticism.

The Grimm Brothers are best known for being one of the first to compile regional folklore, but they were also interested in reconstructing the pre-Christian identity of ancient Germany. While their methodologies were not perfect, they sparked the field we now call European Studies. This concerned the Norse gods because the Grimm Brothers tied the Germanic past to the Scandinavian past on the basis of language similarities, believing that they could fill in Germany's missing history using Norse history. As a result, many German thinkers became interested in the Norse gods.

Objective attempts at the reconstruction of Norse Paganism were plagued by the rosy mists of Romanticism that infatuated Europe at the time. As a result, many things about Norse Paganism were... well, romanticized. For example, Freyja was imagined as the Nordic equivalent of Venus or Aphrodite and depicted as a goddess of beauty, love, lust, and femininity in the same way that the Romans interpreted and portrayed these things. (The Swedish Romantic movement, however, focused more on depicting Freyja as the pining and weeping lover of her long-lost husband.)

Freyja, as well as many of the other Norse gods, reappeared within the greater popular culture in the form of Richard Wagner's *Der Ring Des Nibelungen*, a four-part opera that was first performed (in part) in the year 1869. The initial performance was of its first movement, "Das Rheingold," which is the only part that features the Norse gods.

Wagner took creative liberties in the way he portrayed the gods. Freyja was cast as Freia, a combination of Freyja herself and the goddess Idunn, the wife of Bragi, who is known for bearing the apples of immortality. (Freyja never had such a role within Norse mythology.) Since then, Freyja has become the subject of many different works of art, evolving into something of a muse for artists and poets alike. Her name also started to reappear in different iterations. For example, she's mentioned within the first stanza of the Danish civil national anthem.

FREYJA TODAY

The 1970s brought the New Age movement to the United States and Europe, and with it came the neo-pagan movement. Since then, Norse gods are once again venerated after nearly a thousand years of obscurity.

There has been renewed interest in the worship of Freyja. Today, she's often viewed as a protector of women and girls, and can be called on to help shield them from domestic abuse. Devotees offer her things such as chocolates in acknowledgment of her association with love and romance, and, of course, she's still linked to sex, fertility, and similar.

Though many people worship Freyja within a Norse Pagan context, she's also worshipped outside this as well. She is sometimes chosen as a matron goddess in Wicca, where practitioners select a male and female deity to represent masculine and feminine principles. She's also worshipped within eclectic pagan practices, in which someone might identify as pagan but not focus on just one pantheon of gods.

In both North American and Scandinavian countries, "Freyja" or "Freya" has grown in popularity as a first name. It's also a name popularly used for farm animals and pets, especially cats.

FREYJA IN POP CULTURE

While she's made appearances in many modern retellings and interpretations of the Norse myths, Freyja has also appeared in spin-offs of these, such as within the Marvel comics and video games like *Age of Mythology, Smite,* and *God of War Ragnarok.*

Freyja in Movies and on TV

Freyja has made a few appearances in movies and on TV shows, either as herself or as inspiration for a character. In an episode of *Nautilus* (2024), the characters travel to Freyja's burial ground looking for her treasure, only to encounter guardians (modern-day valkyries). Perhaps the Oseberg burial ship (see page 82) inspired this scene, but it is reasonable to assume that if Freyja had a burial ground, it would be full of her treasures, including the gems and jewelry mentioned in the show.

Freyja also appears to have inspired a character in *The Vampire Diaries* (2008–2017), which features a powerful witch called Freya from the Viking Age. As well as the similarities to witches, *völur,* and Freyja, there is also a connection to fertility, as her birth is a result of a deal to help her barren mother conceive.

Chapter 5: Venerating Freyja

This chapter provides options and avenues for venerating Freyja. Nothing here is required by any means; these suggestions are simply different approaches that Heathens take when venerating, worshipping, or otherwise working with this figure.

HOW TO VENERATE FREYJA

This guide focuses on the development of an interpersonal working relationship with a deity without the involvement of a mediator or doctrine.

Faith—the concept of believing in something without evidence—is also not required. I offer this approach because devotional polytheism can be tailored to one's existing personal philosophies regarding the nature of divinity, which makes it suitable for anyone, no matter what their current perspective may be.

That being said, it's important to understand something of the background from which the Old Norse religions grew, to better understand how Norse deities like Freyja function. As a decentralized worldview, that of the Norse is said to have been animistic in nature. While animism is typically defined as "everything having a soul," this definition is based on the way animism looks within the framework of Christianity, rather than outside it.

Within the context of Norse Paganism, animism can be defined as the acknowledgment of the interconnected nature of all things, and the view that everything, material and immaterial, operates as an ecosystem. The divine and the mundane are not considered separate from one another, nor opposites of each other. As a result, the concept of "sin" does not apply here either—there is no circumstance that draws one closer to or farther away from Freyja. Similarly, there is no set of morals or values we must hold to worship her, nor any other prerequisites whatsoever.

The gods are characterized as being human, but their humanity has taken on epic proportions. This also means that they're not perfect. They have distinct personalities, opinions, and outlooks that we may or may not agree with. When going into a veneration practice with Freyja, think of it as if you're establishing a new interpersonal relationship, complete with the interval of "getting to know someone." What the relationship between you and Freyja looks like, however, is entirely up to you and Freyja.

BUILDING AN ALTAR

Popular among Norse Heathens globally is the act of building an altar or dedicated shrine to a deity. An altar is just as much for you as it is for the deity—a communal space for both of you—and being a part of your living space, it should be something you are happy with.

Some pagans make a distinction between an altar and a shrine, in which case an altar is a space for any kind of crafting or spellwork, whereas a shrine operates as more of a dedicated spot for a deity, ancestor, spirit, or multiple powers. Other pagans do not differentiate, and may use the term "altar" to describe a shrine or a multipurpose space that serves the function of both. For the sake of this passage, I will be using "altar" in the multipurpose sense.

Altars generally operate as a space where offerings are given to powers, and are decorated in ways reminiscent of those powers. They may also house the tools that people use in their practice. Altars can be big or small, simple or complex. They can be placed anywhere, for example on a windowsill or bookshelf, in a shoebox, on a table, on a floating shelf, or even in a virtual space. I have heard of people building temples for their deities in Minecraft servers, or creating websites that serve as digital altars. Other clever ways to create altars include scrapbooking or creating a shadow-box similar to a diorama. In this way, altars can be overt or covert, and tailored to your space and needs.

Some people like to take a very historical approach to altars and put them outdoors. Groves were thought to be sacred spaces in the ancient past, so anyone with a backyard or outside space may take the opportunity to build one out there.

How an altar is decorated is up to the individual. Most people have a spot on the altar where they can make offerings. Altars may also feature some form of iconography of the deity, whether in the form of two-dimensional art or a three-dimensional sculpture. Decorative aspects, such as candles, lights, garlands, altar cloths, or stones, may also be added.

Some altars are thematic and play hard into the Viking theme, with animal pelts and drinking horns, while others are more contemporary in appearance. Others are themed according to the personality of the deity to whom they are dedicated.

An altar should bring you joy in its function as a devotional space. If approaching your altar strikes you with a sense of apprehension or spiritual obligation, you could try rearranging it to be more personable, or even test out a different format

BLÓT, OR OFFERINGS

Blót (pronounced "bloat") means "offering" or "blessing," and describes the giving of a gift. The act of making offerings to a deity is referred to as performing *blót*.

Sometimes *blót* has been mistranslated as meaning "blood," in the sense of offering blood sacrifice, but this is a false etymology. Similarly, the translation of the word into "sacrifice" somewhat misrepresents what *blót* is all about.

While an offering is a sacrifice in the sense that it is something that is given, the term "sacrifice" suggests trial or difficulty; that the harder it is to give something up, the more valuable it is as an offering. It may be tempting to create something extravagant or expensive for Freyja as a way to show dedication to her, and to demonstrate that we're willing to sacrifice a great amount of time, energy, and effort at our own expense to serve the deities we love. However this image of "sacrifice" runs contrary to a lot of Scandinavian cultural concepts around reciprocity. Generally, the Norse gods would not want us to perform acts in their name that are detrimental to our own wellbeing.

Instead, the way in which an offering is typically made in Heathenry is in the spirit of *frith*. This word is often crudely translated to mean "peace," but more accurately describes the state that emerges from mutually enjoyed companionship. Giving gifts in *frith* is the act of giving from a place of human connection, which means that it should be an enjoyable experience for all those who are involved.

HOW TO MAKE AN OFFERING

There are a few general steps to follow when making an offering, which ensure you evoke the correct deity, and not an impostor, and offer something that they would appreciate.

There are many different ways to give an offering to Freyja. Some people make offerings in a formal manner, while others do so more casually. Some people make offerings on a routine basis, while others make them whenever the mood strikes. It really all boils down to your personal preference.

That being said, it's usually common courtesy to give offerings when asking for favors from Freyja, as well as after that favor has been fulfilled. It's also good manners to offer something when you're first introducing yourself to her. Holiday offerings are also popular, particularly when there's already ample food that can be shared, or when it's a holiday that Freyja is especially associated with.

While Freyja has her favorite offering items, she will enjoy any offering so long as it's made with love and honesty.

Here are the steps for making an offering to Freyja:

1

DECIDE WHAT IT IS YOU WANT TO OFFER

Usual offerings consist of food and/or drink, but offerings of trinkets, artwork, poetry, songs, scents, and other gifts also count (for a list of suggestions, see pages 100–102). What you offer doesn't have to be elaborate or "traditional." It's more important that it's heartfelt and genuine. Half a candy bar can be just as meaningful as a fancy home-cooked meal if it is given in the spirit of friendship.

You also don't have to offer a lot of whatever it is. Goddesses like Freyja don't necessarily need to eat the same quantities that we do. I offer what generally fits into an average dipping-sauce bowl, and also have a small drinking horn on a stand for libations. Some Heathens have dedicated crockery and cutlery for offerings, while others simply use what's available in their home kitchen.

2

CLEANSE, BLESS, AND CONSECRATE YOUR OFFERING MATERIALS

This is something that'll make the offering more appetizing. Not only do you want to make sure that your offering materials are clean, they also need to be cleansed.

Cleansing can be thought of as prepping the energy of the material in the same way that cleaning preps the body of the material. Cleansing can be as simple as running the dishes you're about to use under water and soap, and imbuing them with the energies of cleanliness. To do this, you put the sensation of "cleanliness" in your hands and into the act of cleaning the dishes. This is what some people characterize as putting an intention into the act.

For any utensils that can't have prolonged exposure to water and dish soap for any reason, the usual method of cleaning and prepping them works just as well. For example, silver can be cleansed during the polishing process, cast iron can be cleansed during the seasoning process, and steel blades can be cleansed during oiling. Simply taking a soft cloth to "wipe away" residual energy can also be effective for cleansing.

During the cleansing process, you may also want to bless and consecrate the material. A blessing puts good tidings into it, while consecrating it is the act of giving it its function. For example, if you are preparing a drinking horn to use as an offering vessel, you can say something like:

"May this offering horn have a long and cared-for existence in its function as an offering vessel for the gods."

Speech is considered a powerful vehicle for imbuing intention into something within Norse practices. Language, however, is actually optional in this. Something can be spoken through the medium of feelings and actions, so long as you're actually communicating with the object rather than merely visualizing your intention in your mind.

The food and/or beverage may also be blessed, if you wish.

3

EVOKE FREYJA

Once you have your offering prepared, it's time to call Freyja to the space. This can be as simple as approaching your altar, saying a few words, and setting the offering upon it. Personally, I like to light candles as a way of drawing attention to the altar, and it also has the benefit of setting the tone for the space.

If you're evoking Freyja for the first time, it's important to consider the reason. Some people approach Freyja for help with magic or romantic matters, while others are looking to work with her on a regular basis and get to know her in an interpersonal sense. Even if you don't know what it is you're looking for, just be honest about it. The gods can handle every kind of reason—there's nothing that they haven't dealt with before.

What you say when you give the offering and how you say it is entirely up to you, though it's good to be honest and polite. Make it clear that you are evoking Freyja and nobody else.

4

GIVE THE OFFERING

There are many ways that offerings can be transported to the deity. For food/drink offerings, you can leave the offering out for a while before disposing of it or consuming it yourself on behalf of Freyja, or, if you are outdoors, you can give the offering directly to the earth or throw it into a burning firepit. It's a good idea not to leave your food offerings out for so long that they spoil or attract pests—I clean mine up after a few hours, and don't leave them for any longer than overnight. If you struggle to clean up food offerings for one reason or another, consider using non-perishable items. If all else fails, water is always a welcome universal offering for any situation.

Non-food offerings, such as artwork, I will present or leave at the altar. If you're dedicating a song, then make sure to evoke the deity that you've dedicated it to before performing.

FREYJA'S FAVORITE OFFERINGS

Like people, deities always enjoy receiving presents. And, like people, they are especially partial to particular presents. While Freyja enjoys receiving all kinds of gifts—and I invite you to explore what they are yourself—there are a few items that she's known to be fond of within the oral traditions.

FOOD

Deities always appreciate food, and Freyja is no exception. She is not a particularly picky eater, so any food works as an offering, so long as it's given from the heart. Here are some options that people tend to turn to when giving food offerings to Freyja:

Meats

The cold climate of northern Europe limits crop production, which means that the Norse people had to rely more heavily on meat to fill their diets compared to other societies dwelling in more fertile areas of the world. As a result, meat was commonly used as an offering to their gods.

Most of the Norse diet consisted of fish and wild game, which both make good offerings for Freyja. But one meat in particular is especially sacred to the Vanir, and that is pork. Since Freyja and her brother Frey both have boars as steeds, this type of meat makes for an especially potent offering.

Pork products can include things such as ham, bacon, and sausage, all of which are acceptable to offer to Freyja. Be sure all pork offerings are cooked thoroughly, since raw pork can pose a health hazard. Any offerings of pork should either be consumed on behalf of the goddess, or disposed of after being left out for no more than an hour. For a less perishable option, pork jerky is a good alternative.

Rations

It's common for people enlisted in the military to offer some of their rations to Freyja in honor of her activities on the battlefield. Unlike Odin, who operates as more of a strategist when it comes to war, Freyja often takes to the front lines, fighting among soldiers and riding with valkyries. Rations are offered to her in honor of this.

Hard Candies

Another great offering for Freyja is hard candies, particularly anything fruity. German hard candies fit the bill nicely, especially since they can be left out longer than perishable foods. Leave some in a bowl on Freyja's altar for her to enjoy!

Homemade Foods

Homemade meals or snacks are valued offerings for any deity, Freyja included. They can be anything from soups, to pies, to breads, to cookies, and more. Making offerings of homemade meals also helps invite deities into the fabric of your life, establishing a place for them within it.

Homemade meals don't have to be lavish. The offering could be a portion of whatever it is you've decided to make for yourself that night, or it could be a

confection you prepare in honor of the deity. In any case, homemade foods are crafted by hand, and therefore creating them is an act of devotion as much as the act of offering itself.

Chocolate

This is a modern offering to Freyja due to her role as a goddess of love and romance. Since cocoa has stimulant properties, chocolate is sometimes believed to work as both a mood-booster and an aphrodisiac, which lends it to associations with love, romance, and sex.

The type of chocolate doesn't necessarily have to be fancy—Freyja accepts all kinds. Chocolate offerings might be anything from a simple bar to chocolate chips, to a fancy box of delicious cocoa treats.

BEVERAGES

Libations have long been given to gods as offerings. Freyja is a fan of many beverages, but a few favorites include:

Beer and Ale

A favorite of warriors and commoners alike, Freyja always enjoys a good beer. This beverage was also historically brewed by women, giving it a further link to Freyja. In the Norse myths, Freyja is depicted as helping the valkyries serve beer to both guests and the einherjar—warriors who die in battle—but that doesn't mean she doesn't sit down and enjoy it herself too. If giving alcoholic offerings is of interest to you, she would always appreciate a good lager.

Mead

This is a traditional offering for the Norse gods. Mead is an alcohol distilled from honey, and is sometimes referred to as honey wine. It was considered a special drink and brought out for important occasions and celebrations. Freyja will always accept a glassful (or hornful) of mead with gratitude.

Coffee

For non-alcoholic offerings, coffee is a good choice for Freyja. She enjoys all kinds of coffee, from mochas and espressos to lattes.

Water

If all else fails, water is a welcome offering for Freyja. While seemingly mundane in comparison to mead or ale, water is actually one of the best universal offerings, and the act of sharing water is one of the oldest gestures of *frith*, or peace, that we have. Freyja appreciates water at any time.

ART AND ACTIVITIES

In addition to food, typical offerings to Norse gods include feats of artistry, skill, and craftsmanship. These don't always have to be the most skilled of creations, and it's more important that they come from a place of genuine feeling. Here are some things often dedicated to Freyja:

Fibercrafts

Fibercraft activities make excellent offerings for Freyja. These can include knitting, crocheting, or even nalbinding, which is a method of creating textiles using a large, flat needle and your thumb that predates both knitting and crochet. It has been used all over the world, especially in northern Europe during the Viking Age.

Other good fibercraft offerings for Freyja include weaving, sewing, embroidery, and yarn-spinning. These activities can also be done in the goddess's presence and as an activity that she can participate in with you.

Magic

For those inclined to do so, learning a magical practice is a great devotional activity to Freyja. She is, after all, the goddess who taught Odin all he knows about seid (see pages 103–109). The kind of magic practiced doesn't necessarily have to be specific to her, but she can be a great help in instruction, support, and learning within your magical endeavors.

Martial Arts

Since Freyja is a war goddess, she's also keen on activities involving self-defense. Learning a martial art can make a great offering for Freyja, and can also be used as a bonding activity to get to know her.

SEID AND PRACTICING SEID

Seid (*seiðr* in Old Norse, pronounced in a similar way to "seether") is a kind of Norse magic for shaping outcomes. It's connected to Norse concepts of fate and destiny, and has additional connections with spinning and the art of weaving.

In the *Ynglinga Saga*, Freyja is said to have brought seid to the Aesir. The poem *Völuspá* loosely attributes this to a figure named Gullveig, who some scholars believe is actually the same figure as Freyja (see page 54). Therefore, since this is an artform attributed to Freyja it is also one she can teach and that can be used to connect with her.

Before this, though, let's take a look at the background of seid.

SEID IN NORSE SOCIETIES

Not much is known about historical seid beyond descriptions of what it can accomplish. We know it existed due to archaeological finds of seid practitioners and their implements, and due to the fact that this art is mentioned in a few medieval Icelandic sagas.

Both men and women practiced seid, with the former being referred to as *seiðmenn* (singular: *seiðmaðr*), and the latter being called *seiðkonur* or *völur* (singular: *seiðkona* or *völva*). However, it was considered taboo for men to practice seid, despite the fact that the god Odin himself practices it. Perhaps this was due to the sexually deviant connotations around seid, or maybe its manipulative nature didn't sit well with the Norse sensibilities of manliness. Either way, we do seem to have more female examples of seid practitioners than male ones.

Norse Seeresses, or Völur

Women who practiced seid were referred to as *völur*. Their skills encompassed acts such as prophesying, divining, communicating with otherworldly beings (including gods, spirits, and the dead), channeling, and, of course, shaping destiny. *Völur* would often roam the countryside, traveling from town to town to offer their services. Most worked by themselves, but some preferred to travel in pairs or groups.

Many *völur* carried a staff made of wood or iron. This tool is where the name *völva* comes from, which means "staff-bearer" in Old Norse. The staffs belonging to *völur* were based on distaffs, which are items normally used for spinning flax into yarn. These were typically the size of a wand or larger, but smaller than a walking stick, and often had a bulb at the top to support the flax. *Völur* staffs weren't typically used for spinning yarn, however, and instead served ornamental purposes.

In many cases, *völur* were respected for their line of work, with some going to the grave richly buried and finely decorated. At other times, they were met with wariness and apprehension due to their capabilities. The occupation began to dwindle as Scandinavia gradually became more Christian, and with time it fell into obscurity altogether.

Seid's Function

Seid was mainly used to shape destiny, but it also had other, broader applications. Practitioners of seid could use it to find things, influence the weather, speak to the dead, shapeshift, summon spirits, and perform mental manipulations. They could also use it to hear prophecies and fortunes and discern hidden information.

Unfortunately for us, there are no surviving instructions for how to practice the ancient forms of seid. However, we do know something about its mechanics. Seid was not something cast or performed, but rather something spun. The art is associated with the act of spinning flax using a spindle and distaff. The distaff holds the fibers of the flax while the spindle is used to spin it into yarn. The action behind this is a pulling one. Seid works via these same operations, through the act of pulling the threads of fate into a focused shape and later weaving that fate into a design.

The Concept of Fate and the Soul in Norse Paganism

The concept of fate in Norse societies was a complex one. In some ways, destiny was portrayed as fixed, while in other ways, it was fluid. All of it was characterized through the Web of Wyrd, with the word "wyrd" relating to the relationship between cause and effect

that creates the circumstances around us. By manipulating the wyrd we can manipulate our circumstances, and thereby change our fate.

The characteristics of fate and its movability can be better understood when we look at the Norse concept of the soul. In Norse cosmology the soul was not a single fixed thing (let alone something that was localized in our bodies), but comprised of multiple parts. Some of these parts are as follows:

Hamr: Our body, or more specifically our shape. This shape includes our physical body, but also things like our presence and comportment. We can change the shape of our *hamr* to a degree, with our *hugr* as the catalyst.

Hugr: Our thoughts or mind. This part can travel out of the body (such as in dreams or while in a state of trance) and take on various shapes.

Fylgja: A "follower" that protects us. It was historically characterized as a guardian of sorts, which took the form of an animal, or, in later traditions, a woman. We can think of our *fylgja* as being the representation of our instincts and mammalian tendencies. We may or may not be aware of our *fylgja* and how it operates in the background of our lives, but it's always working hard to protect us and keep us safe.

Hamingja: Once considered an entity that personified our luck in life, in modern terms *hamingja* can be thought of as the circumstances we inherit, including things such as genetics, wealth, connections, and the opportunities available by virtue of our environment. "Family curses" can also be part of the *hamingja*.

In terms of shaping destiny, we can't go back and rework our *hamingja*; this part of us more or less represents where we stand within the Web of Wyrd. But that doesn't mean we can't modify it going forward by weaving the wyrd into outcomes we wish to see.

The wyrd weaves itself whether we have a hand in it or not, and left to its own devices it is what we deem to be natural law or causation. The Norse, however, portrayed these forces as being the work of entities known as Norns, women who spin the destinies of all things (see page 20). Not even the gods are immune to the work of the Norns, and they have had to learn seid in the same way humans do in order to alter the course of destiny.

MODERN SEID

Since there is so little information on the actual methods involved in practicing seid, its modern forms are interpretations based on what we do know about seid historically. Modern forms generally have a shamanic quality, since seid had functions similar to many shamanistic practices, and can incorporate things like drumming, chanting, or veiling—the act of covering the head and face to put weight on the head and block out all light, which helps with trance practices (see page 109).

Sometimes seid is practiced during elaborate rituals, and other times it's performed casually and without prior preparation. Since seid is within Freyja's purview, it can be used to connect more deeply with her, and she can help those who wish to dive deeper into the practice.

IS SEID EVIL OR DANGEROUS?

Seid is a methodology for shaping outcomes. In other words, it's a tool. And like any tool, what makes it beneficial or harmful lies in how a person chooses to use it.

As far as danger goes, the only real dangers with seid have to do with the manifestation of outcomes, especially outcomes involved in shaping other people. Any parent whose child grew up to resent them can tell you this. Be aware that our treatment of other people contributes to shaping them and their destinies; we otherwise won't go into how to do this. Shaping others is a complicated business that has a lot of ethical considerations. What's more, it cannot be done successfully if we can't shape ourselves first.

Beyond this, the nature of learning seid is otherwise very similar to learning how to knit. Just as with knitting, we'll make mistakes in how we weave our circumstances and have to learn how to fix those mistakes. But the good news is that actions—even the ones we don't intend to take—are only ever going to result in their natural outcomes. In other words, we don't incur any additional karmic debt for messing up. The price of the mistake is the cost of it.

HOW TO PRACTICE SEID

Seid is an art, and like any art, we need to practice it to become good at it. Skill with seid is not an inherent ability that we can learn to tap into. It also doesn't work by simply willing an outcome into existence. It works by manipulating the mechanics behind how things move. There are three things we need to know in order to do this: The pattern of how a thing moves; what influences that pattern; and how to influence it ourselves.

There are many interpretations of how to practice seid. The following pages offer a few different approaches that you might like to try. No matter how you practice seid, you can always call upon Freyja for help. You can discover more about communicating with her on page 111.

The Cycle of Training the Senses

I've found that seid makes more sense when we've prepared ourselves for it. Seid operates through a very old and very kinesthetic form of thinking, which is actually the same sense we use to sail masted ships: We use the feel of the wind and sails in relation to the ship to navigate it across water. However, most of us don't incorporate this kinesthetic sense into our ways of thinking these days, and instead we think mostly in words, pictures, or calculations.

To shape destiny, we need to relearn how to think kinesthetically. The best way to describe how this feels is that the mental information we process takes the form of a motion-like feeling inside our bodies. Getting back to this will help you to construct the essential foundations of understanding seid.

Step 1: Resourcing the Mind

Why are we talking about the mind if seid is something felt within the body? It's because motion is interpreted by the mind just as much as it's felt by the body, and unlike with masted ships, we can't rely on actual haptic feedback to help us measure the wyrd. This sensation of feeling circumstances move is experienced on the inside rather than the outside. This means we need to be able to measure the sensations inside our bodies to a heightened degree, which requires building up our personal awareness.

Awareness is the degree to which we understand our own actions and behaviors and where they come from. One of the best ways to raise awareness is through mindfulness meditation. This is a method of looking at our thoughts impartially while immersing our brains in an oxygen-rich environment. The more we do this, the deeper we can go into our minds, and therefore the deeper we can then go into our bodies.

Self-awareness is different from self-reflection. The purpose of this is to become comfortable within our own presence rather than reflecting on our behaviors or reasons.

Step 2: Connecting to the Body

Many people are of the mind that spiritual enlightenment comes from transcending the human form or "rising above the ape." But with seid, the exact opposite is true. Our knowledge of everything deepens when we go deeper into the body.

Connection with the body arises as a result of becoming familiar with it. If we spend our days going through the same motions in life, we're going to start losing connection with our bodies. This is true even if we're always having different experiences. After all, touring a foreign city or visiting a new store still uses the same stock-motions we use to pilot ourselves through our daily routines.

To strengthen our kinesthetic sense, we need to break our bodies out of these stock-motions. The goal is to give our bodies new and novel kinesthetic experiences daily, in the same way that we give ourselves new and novel visual and auditory experiences daily.

The nice thing about this is that we don't need to change our routine to achieve it. We just have to find new ways to enjoy the things we already do. So, as you go about your day, try to use your body in ways you haven't before. Let's say you're making coffee in the morning. Instead of just going through the motions of making coffee, try to actively make your movements different somehow and really engage with that difference. Apply this to any activity you do when you think of it. Breaking out of our stock-motions and making them different may feel weird and even unnatural at first, but it gets less weird the more you do it.

Step 3: Pattern Awareness

As you cultivate both your mind and body for seid, you may start to notice patterns a lot more than before. Much of this will be information you already subconsciously picked up on but just weren't aware of before.

At this stage, all you really have to concern yourself with is noticing patterns of outcomes and the forces that cause them. You'll also want to pay attention to any time you find yourself theorizing about why things are occurring. It's better to wait until you know for sure what's causing something, before drawing conclusions about what's going on.

Step 4: Pattern Application

At this point you can change your actions to see if they change the results you see in life.

For example, as you go to make coffee in the morning, try grabbing the cup with your non-dominant hand, or try interrupting yourself in the middle of a task as you're doing it. It may feel frustrating and weird at first, but the more you do it the easier it'll become.

Note that this process isn't strictly linear. We can work on steps 3 and 4 at the same time we're working on steps 1 and 2. Be sure to treat the process as one that continuously cycles through your life, rather than a list of tasks to complete.

Practicing Seid through Fibercrafts

Recall that seid is understood through a very kinesthetic sense and is the same sense used for sailing masted ships. It's also used in another, more commonplace activity: Fibercrafts. Whether the medium is knitting, crochet, loom knitting, or something else, we can use fibercrafts to train our kinesthetic senses.

Fibercrafts work for this because the knowledge of how to weave is stored in the body. By weaving, we can become familiar with the shape of how things move. After all, the movement of the wyrd is reflected in knitting; repeating a certain behavior in life is like repeating a stitch. Repeating the same action over and over again creates the same result, in the same way that repeating a stitch over and over again creates the same result. But just as we train our bodies to make different movements through knitting, so we can train our minds to adopt different behaviors in life. This permeates into everything we do.

It doesn't matter too much what kind of fibercrafts you take up, but if you want to try a historical form, the Norse people used to practice a very old technique known as nalbinding. This is a form of knitting which used a single needle.

Practicing Seid through Trance or Meditation

Another way seid can be practiced is through meditation or trancework. By looking inward, we can look outward. Many modern-day seid practitioners do this through activities like drumming, or by covering their heads with a dark cloth.

Start by putting on some music that helps your mind wander and clearing the space around you. Dim or turn off the lights. Place a heavy blanket or cloth over your head. As you listen to the music, let your body sway and move as it wishes in time to the music—what this does is help take our inner judge offline and open our minds to spiritual perceptions.

While you settle into this rhythm, let your mind wander through the current circumstances of your life. You can do this through visualization, through feeling, or through recalling the interactions you've had. Try to map out the network of how these circumstances interrelate to create a sense of your life's landscape.

You may notice that life is not a linear sequence of events, but rather an ecosystem of cause and effect. You may also find that the landscape of your life is not a fixed thing, but rather something defined by movement. When we become aware of what our life is doing and how it moves, we gain more and more power to change it.

You can replace the music used in trancework with drumming if you wish. Some people also drink a mugwort tea beforehand to facilitate the experience (consult your doctor first if you are nursing, pregnant, or allergic to ragweed).

Practicing Seid through Divination

Seid has been used for divinatory purposes since the Viking Age. The poem *Völuspá* consists of a prophecy a seeress gave to Odin through divination. This divination was likely done through trancework or channeling, but naturally we can practice seid using any form of divination method that pleases us; the medium itself doesn't matter too much, so long as it serves its purpose.

If you don't want to try to divine through trancework, you can use a method such as tarot or rune-reading to get a picture of the landscape of your life. You can do this by asking questions about the nature of certain events and their outcomes. This will help you gain a better understanding of how things ended up the way they did, and why.

It helps to keep a journal recording your readings. The way I do this is by drawing three columns. In the first column I write the question asked and the name of the card or rune I pulled that answered it. In the second column I write my initial interpretation of the card/rune and what it means in relation to my question. After some time has passed and my head is clearer, I reinterpret the answer and write it down in the third column.

FREYJA'S SPECIAL DAYS

Many of the Norse deities have special days or even holidays associated with them, which make for potent times to work with them or make offerings.

FRIDAY

Most of the names for the days of the week, with the exception of Saturday, are derived from the Norse gods. Friday comes from both Frigg and Freyja, which originates from the Old Norse *frjá-dagr*. The modern Scandinavian variation of this word is *fredag* (in Norwegian, Swedish, and Danish), though in Faroese it's *fríggjadagur*. These all mean "Freyja's day," which makes Friday a perfect day for any veneration involving Freyja. Friday the 13th is especially potent for working with Freyja, since 13 is a number that's sacred to her.

SPRING EQUINOX AND MIDSUMMER

Due to Freyja's association with fertility, she was often venerated during spring and summertime holidays across northern Europe. The traditions associated with these celebrations vary depending on the locality, so there is no universal set holiday. However, the spring equinox and midsummer have become holidays associated with Freyja and her brother Frey, given their ties to abundance.

COMMUNICATING WITH FREYJA

Some people are content with worshipping a deity without any additional interaction outside this. Others may want to experience a greater degree of socialization with them.

This section will go over the general basics of spirit and deity work, and give you different methods and tools that may help you in that journey.

SOME THINGS TO CONSIDER

It's very easy to get caught up in the glamor of deity work due to its "mystical" and "supernatural" nature. But these relationships work in very much the same way that mundane ones do:

You Will Still Need to Get to Know Freyja

I've watched many of my fellow pagans get caught off-guard because they confused knowing a lot about a god with having personal familiarity. No matter how much you know through research, please be prepared to learn more through your interactions.

Relationship Dynamics Matter

What's healthy in mundane interpersonal relationships is also healthy in spiritual ones, and what's unhealthy in mundane interpersonal relationships is equally unhealthy in spiritual ones.

Deities Are Not Mind Readers

Deities can have a better understanding of how we might be thinking and feeling than most people, but that doesn't mean they can read minds, or see a record of everything we've ever thought. Gods won't know what we're thinking unless we communicate our thoughts to them.

Deity Work Takes Effort

Along with everything that comes with maintaining any relationship, deity work involves researching, learning new tools of communication, discovering new skills, and accepting that there will be a process of trial and error.

The Relationship Is Between You and the Deity

It bodes ill if someone is acting as a dedicated "interpreter" between you and Freyja, since this can prevent you from having agency and confidence in your spiritual relationships.

You Can Say "No"

Just because Freyja may want something or suggest something, it doesn't mean you have to go along with it.

Gods Can Say "No"

Gods are not wish-granting machines into which we can load prayers until a miracle pops out. Freyja may not want or be able to manifest a circumstance for one reason or another.

Incompatibility Happens

Sometimes a deity's personality, methods, and antics might not vibe well with you. That's okay. We just need to recognize when this happens and make adjustments accordingly.

METHODS OF COMMUNICATION

Communicating with Freyja can happen through many modalities. The more methods of communication you use, the more methods of confirmation you are likely to experience. It's best to use many different kinds of communication, rather than to rely on just one.

SYNCHRONICITIES

Synchronicities are signs and portents that signal the presence of a deity. They can manifest as dreams or even as physical phenomena. Synchronicities can be thought of as "coincidences that seem far too convenient to be simply coincidental," and they often come in multiples. They are characterized by having an air of uncanniness about them, and usually appear when you least expect them to.

It's important to keep the concept of "multiples" in mind when it comes to synchronicities. Seeing a cat on your way to school or work may not necessarily be a sign from Freyja in and of itself... but having cats show up in random places; seeing a falcon, hawk, or other bird of prey; having dreams about Freyja; sensing her presence; and having her name come up in conversations, all when we least expect it—these may indicate something.

Probability plays a role in this as well. If you know birds of prey live nearby, then seeing one may not necessarily be a sign from Freyja. However, spotting one out of nowhere and having it grab your attention in some way may. It's the fact that the signs are unusual and move in ways that fall outside the normal rhythm of life that make them what they are.

Synchronicities are helpful because they provide a way for a deity to tell you who they are in ways that are unique to them. Sometimes the delivery is as telling as the sign itself, and can help you clue in not just on who the deity is, but that they are, in fact, who they say they are.

DIVINATION

Along with its use for fortune telling, divination can be used to facilitate communication with Freyja. After evoking her, you can use a divination method such as runes, tarot or an oracle deck, cartomancy, or dice divination to ask questions and receive answers.

In order to make sure you have the deity you think you do, you can conduct a deity interview spread (see opposite). This is also a good way to make sure who you have is authentic, as opposed to an impostor spirit (see page 118). The spread was designed for tarot, but can be used with other mediums as well.

Divination methods that have a greater degree of random chance, such as tarot or runes, are generally good for verification because it's a lot harder for us to subconsciously influence the results. Divination methods that are easier for us to influence, such as pendulums, aren't as reliable.

Sometimes it's difficult to figure out in the moment what a reading is saying, but recording it means you can go back and check again at a later time when your mind is clear.

DEITY INTERVIEW SPREAD

1. Who are you? This card identifies the spirit, deity, or entity in question. This roughly corresponds to how the entity sees themselves.

2. What are you known for? Think of this as the entity's history or background.

3. Name one of your traits. This is a characteristic, feature, or quality that the entity has.

4. Name one of your skills. This is a skill, talent, or area of specialization that the entity has.

5. What is something you're associated with? This can be an event, a symbolic image, or a concept that is attributed to the entity.

CLAIRSENSES

The clairsenses or "clear-senses" are characterized as perceptions that are roughly equivalent to our physical ones, correlating to our senses of smell, taste, hearing, touch, and sight. It's thought that clairsenses measure metaphysical stimuli rather than material ones, and therefore can be used to interact with deities in a way that's similar to interacting with anyone else.

I find this model can be misleading because clairsenses, like "clairvoyance" (clear-seeing) or "clairsentience" (clear-thinking), are rather abstract. It also risks giving the impression that training the clairsenses is about training the physical senses to perceive metaphysical information about the world, which can actually have negative consequences.

Communicating with deities and spirits is, fortunately, a much simpler process—it's about becoming aware of what our inner senses are already detecting. I say "inner senses," because noticing what our clairsenses are doing is a byproduct of directing our awareness inward.

Establishing a connection with Freyja through our clairsenses creates a direct channel of perception and communication where conversations can be exchanged in real time. That being said, how our minds experience this kind of thing is different for everyone. It's important to recognize how clairsenses manifest as sensations within yourself.

Note that our ability to perceive the inner senses can be clouded by many things—our emotions, our imaginations, symptoms of mental ailments, or even an overworked nervous system. We need to use discernment at every turn and avoid taking everything at face value. Even when we are able to identify our clairsenses, discernment is still important for things such as differentiating gods from impostor spirits (see pages 116–118).

A COURAGE RITUAL WITH FREYJA

This ritual is designed to help facilitate your connection with Freyja and learn how to incorporate her within a meditation practice. For this ritual, we will be calling on Freyja to help build our sense of courage, but "courage" here can be replaced with anything else you'd like Freyja to help you with.

WHAT YOU'LL NEED

- A quiet space
- A tea candle, real or electric
- Energy-cleansing spray, which you can make by filling a spray bottle with water and adding some dried mint
- Mugwort, either as a bundle or as mugwort tea (consult your doctor first if you are nursing, pregnant, or have allergies to ragweed)
- A water offering for Freyja (see *How to Make an Offering*, pages 97–99)
- Music to help you meditate (optional)

HEALTH AND SAFETY

- Never leave a lit bundle unattended.
- Always stay near a source of water in case you must quickly extinguish a flame.

PART 1: PREPARATIONS

1. Light the candle for Freyja to create a sense of sacred space.

2. Banish any stagnant energy in the room by spraying the energy-cleansing spray all around.

3. Light the mugwort bundle until there's a good flame, then blow it out so it fumes, letting the scent fill the space. If you are using tea, drink your mugwort tea instead. This can help you get into the right frame of mind.

4. Sit in a comfortable position in front of the lit candle with your back straight. You can be cross-legged or sitting in a chair, just so long as your back is in a straight and comfortable position.

5. If you know how to, call in your spirit guides to help with the meditation.

Next, call in Freyja. You can do this by saying the following:

"I call forth the lady of the Vanir
I call forth the lady of gold
I call forth the lady of the falcon cloak
I call forth the lady of the slain
I call forth the lady of protection
I call forth the lady of beauty
I call forth the lady of love
I call forth the lady of war
I call forth the lady of death
I call forth the lady of mysteries
I call forth the lady of childbirth
I call forth the lady of womanhood
I call forth the lady of magic
I call forth the lady of Brisingamen
I call forth Freyja to be here please
I call forth Freyja to be here please
I call forth Freyja to be here please"

At this point, there should be a shift of energy in the room as Freyja enters.

7. Ask Freyja for assistance in helping guide you toward courage.

PART 2: ENTERING THE MEDITATION

1. As you sit and drink your tea (if using), think of a time when you have felt courage, then either visualize that memory or recreate the feeling in your body. Let Freyja help guide you to this.

2. Take slow, deep breaths. Allow each breath you take in to amplify the feeling of courage and each breath out to settle deeper into the feeling.

3. Do this for 5 or 10 minutes. Afterward, pace yourself in 5-minute increments to see how you're doing. Don't go for longer than 30 minutes because you will need to give your back a break.

4. Once you feel full of courage, let yourself sink down into a feeling of gratitude. Thank Freyja for the courage and let her know that you've finished.

PART 3: EXITING THE MEDITATION

1. At this point, imagine yourself placing a little bit of that courage at the base of Yggdrasil, the World Tree. If you cannot visualize this, then simply go through the motions with your hands of setting that courage beneath the base of the tree.

2. Dismiss your spirit guides, remembering to thank them.

3. Close the sacred space by blowing out/turning off the candle.

4. Clean up anything that needs cleaning and tidying.

5. Have a snack to ground yourself if need be, or do something that returns you to daily life.

THE TOOLS OF DISCERNMENT

There are many different tools of discernment. Practicing them and strengthening them will help you to build accuracy and clarity in all your spiritual perceptions.

Discernment is the act of differentiating what something is from what we think it is, as well as from what it's not. When you smell a carton of milk to check if it's spoiled, you're using discernment.

THE SANDBOX

Aristotle once famously said, "It is the mark of an educated mind to be able to entertain a thought without accepting it." This is the function of what I call the sandbox. The sandbox is a space or container in your mind where all new information goes, where you can play with it without necessarily accepting it as part of your worldview.

It allows us to consider our experiences before deciding how to interpret them. For example, if we see a cat and believe it's a sign from Freyja, we need to be able to stop and ask ourselves, "Is this belief a result of the experience or a reflection of my desire for a sign?"

The sandbox is not the tool to reveal that answer to us. Rather, it's where we can "hold that thought" until we gather more information.

DISAMBIGUATION

Disambiguation is the act of telling things apart, usually by comparing and contrasting them.

Imagine you have a basket full of different kinds of apples in front of you, and you want to find the Honeycrisp. You know that a Honeycrisp has a red-yellow skin, so you easily rule out the green Granny Smith and the Red Delicious. You are left with apples that look similar, so now you use a different method to tell them apart; you might consider pattern or texture, or even start biting into them to taste-test. We can run comparisons until we have a clear idea of what it is we're looking at.

Disambiguation is something you can turn to in instances when you're not sure whether a deity is actually who they say they are, or if you're not sure whether what you're experiencing is an energy or an emotional reaction, or if you can't tell whether the dream you had was an anxiety/desire or premonition.

NOTICING

In order for us to discern things, we first need to make sure we're actually noticing them. Notice, for example, how your body is positioned. Notice yourself reading the words on these pages. With enough practice, it's possible to even notice ourselves during moments of intense anger or sadness; we "float" above our emotions and observe them even in the middle of having them.

Noticing allows us to examine the things we are perceiving, regardless of the thoughts or feelings we have in relation to them. This is important for perceiving the inner senses because it allows us to interpret them accurately, as opposed to interpreting things the way we wish them to be.

CONFIRMATION BIAS

This is less of a discernment tool and more of a phenomenon to be aware of. Confirmation bias is defined as "the tendency to search for, interpret, favor, and recall information that confirms or supports your prior personal beliefs or values." In other words, it's the act of finding evidence to support your beliefs rather than basing your beliefs on evidence.

It's hard not to have hopes for certain outcomes with deity and spirit work, but finding evidence to support our hopes will not guarantee their manifestation; it will only support the story we have in our minds. The more you work against confirmation bias, the more authentic your interactions with Freyja will be.

ON DEITY WORK AND MENTAL ILLNESS

Some people wonder how to tell the difference between clairsenses and the manifestation of preexisting mental ailments, and whether these two things can coexist at all. The answer is that it really just depends. As a general rule, though, I always recommend checking in with yourself about how you're doing as you go, by asking yourself:

- Is this work interfering with my day-to-day life?
- Is this causing me distress, anxiety, confusion, or disruption in any way?
- Am I having a hard time with discernment in general right now?

If your practice is giving you undue distress, then it may be good to set some boundaries with it. As intriguing as deity work is, your sense of stability in the world comes first.

MENTAL SOCK PUPPETS

A mental "sock puppet" is the result of you talking to yourself and interpreting that self-talk as an entity. Here are some signs you might be dealing with a mental sock puppet:

- It acts in accordance with your whims and expectations.
- You receive no "new" or unique information from interacting with the sock puppet.
- The sock puppet is only as knowledgeable as you are.

- It has no autonomous nature (it only abides by your will).
- It gives no portents or signs unless you're looking for them.

Mental sock puppets only exist for as long as we use them, and the way to stop using them is to draw our awareness to their existence.

IMPOSTORS

Not all entities may be what they seem, and it's possible to encounter things that look like Freyja but, in fact, are not, especially if this is your first foray into deity work. That's why it's important to check to make sure you have the entity you think you have before committing.

It's possible for petty spirits to impersonate deities for their own gain. These impostor spirits are more opportunists than are actual threats.

A simple way to make sure you have the real Freyja is to deliberately evoke her. That, and warding your space (see right). Impostors usually aren't professional actors and can be spotted by a number of telltale behaviors. Some of these behaviors are red-flag actions, such as:
- They refuse to let you interact with other entities or people, or do further research on them.
- They claim they can give you everything you want, preying on your insecurities, desires, and ego.
- They rush you into oaths or vows.
- They're vague about who they are.
- They don't recognize you even if you've had prior interactions with them.

Since impostors are looking for "low-risk, high-rewards," they usually don't like getting caught.

WARDING

Warding is the act of creating a certain set of permissions and allowances for your space. To begin warding, first cleanse your space. This can be as simple as cleaning it with the intention of moving the energy, or using something like smoke cleansing or another method to get rid of any stagnant energy.

Wards need a minimum of three things: Instructions to follow; a battery to be powered by (such as a crystal charged in the sun); and a way to be attached to the space you're in (such as a wand or your finger). Say your instructions out loud as you string your intention around the room with your finger or wand, starting with your battery and working your way back to it, like a circuit.

You can write your instructions as a list first if you'd like. Make sure to keep it as reference and so you can boost your wards later if they become stagnant. Be clear about what your wards should do, such as whether they should only allow certain entities to enter and/or if they should kick out any entities for not obeying particular house rules (which you also specify). Always make sure that only you can change the behavior and instructions of your wards.

CLOSING NOTES ON HEATHENRY

As you make your way into a veneration practice with Freyja, consider these final words on the ongoing evolution of Norse polytheism...

Throughout this book, I mention "Heathenry" and "Norse Paganism." As of now, these appear to be the most common descriptors when referring to neo-pagan practices and beliefs inspired by, or derived from, the folkloric customs, practices, and beliefs of the pre-Christian societies of the Nordic countries. What makes them different is subject to interpretation.

Currently, Heathenry is undergoing rapid growth and development, with many people gravitating toward it. Perhaps the most common question I am asked by others is: "How do I become a Heathen?" I want to take a moment to address this... or rather, to address the assumption that "being Heathen" is a matter of following instructions or conforming to a set of values or ideals.

Many people who come to this practice assume that Norse Paganism is performed in the same way we bake a cake—that a Heathen practice is a product of adding all the right ingredients. This is not the case. Rather, it is something more like a garden: It grows out of the space around us and the architecture of our lives.

Functionally speaking, this doesn't mean you have to follow certain instructions in order to be rewarded with an interpersonal relationship with Freyja. Instead, your interpersonal relationship grows out of trying different ways to venerate her and figuring out what's best for you.

Regardless of our path and regardless of what we may call ourselves, the heart of spirituality is to find what works best for us by trying many different things.

GLOSSARY

In this book, I've chosen to use anglicized versions of the Old Norse names (with the exception of Freyja). Other books, however, may use the Old Norse. The glossary below gives both versions as well as a rough guide to pronunciation.

PRONUNCIATION OF OLD NORSE & ICELANDIC LETTERS

A, a	"Ah" as in "l<u>a</u>va"	Ó, ó	"O" as in "<u>o</u>val" or "b<u>oa</u>t"
Á, á	"Ow" as in "<u>ow</u>l" or "<u>ouch</u>" or "<u>aw</u>l"	Ö, ö	"Uh" as in "<u>e</u>nough"
Æ, æ	"Aye" as in "<u>eye</u>" or "m<u>igh</u>t"	Ǫ, ǫ	Same as ö
Ð, ð	Voiced "th" as in "<u>th</u>at" or "<u>th</u>e"	Œ, œ	Same as ö
É, é	"Yeh" as in "<u>ye</u>t"	Ú, ú	"Oo" as in "m<u>oo</u>d" or "r<u>u</u>de" or "l<u>oo</u>t"
I, i	"Ih" as in "<u>i</u>nn" or "b<u>i</u>n"	Ý, ý	Same as í
Í, í	"Ee" as in "<u>ee</u>l" or "<u>ee</u>rie"	Þ, þ	Unvoiced "th" as in "<u>th</u>ing" or "<u>th</u>aw"
J, j	"Ye" as in "<u>y</u>ard" or "<u>y</u>our"		

A NOTE ABOUT "-R"

The "r" at the end of words such as "Jörmungandr" and "Óðr" are not fully pronounced. The trick is to start saying the letter and then "give up" halfway through.

GODS, GODDESSES, GIANTS, AND OTHER IMPORTANT FIGURES

English	Old Norse	
Bayun		The name of the father cat who sired Freyja's cats according to Russian folklore.
Fenrir		The wolf who swallows Odin during Ragnarok.
Frey	Freyr	A warrior who traded his sword for his wife. He is associated with fertility, prosperity, masculinity, and kingship.
Freyja		A powerful and beautiful goddess. She is associated with love, beauty, magic, and war.
Frigg		The Allmother. She is associated with weaving, wisdom, and women's mysteries.

Gef		A name attributed to Freyja, meaning "she who gives prosperity and happiness."
Gefjun	Gefjon	A goddess who turned her four sons into bulls and plowed the gulf between Denmark and Sweden.
Gerd	Gerðr	A lovely *jötun* and wife of the god Frey.
Gersemi		Daughter of Od and Freyja.
Gullinbursti		Frey's golden boar.
Gullveig		A female figure who was killed three times by the Aesir and reborn each time, becoming a powerful seeress afterward.
Heid	Heiðr	The name Gullveig takes on after she is reborn three times.
Heimdall	Heimdallr	The watchman of Asgard.
Hildisvini	Hildisvíni	Freyja's boar.
Hnoss		Daughter of Od and Freyja.
Hoenir	Hœnir	Odin's brother, who was traded to the Vanir during hostage negotiations.
Horn	Hörn	A name of unknown origin connected to the goddess Freyja. It potentially means "flaxen."
Hyndla		A giantess that Freyja tricks into revealing Ottar's (Freyja's lover) ancestry.
Jormungand	Jörmungandr	The World Serpent, who encircles the Earth.
Loki		Asgard's resident mischief-maker.
Mardoll	Mardöll	A name for Freyja, meaning "one who illuminates the sea" or "one who makes the sea swell."
Mimir	Mímir	The embalmed head of a wise giant. Odin consults it as an oracle.
Njord	Njörðr	Father of Frey and Freyja, and associated with the sea. Uncomfortably married to Skadi.
Odin	Oðinn	The Allfather. Chief of the Aesir and associated with wisdom, war, poetry, madness, and death.
Od	Óðr	Freyja's absent husband. She travels the world in search of him.
Ottar		Freyja's lover.
Skadi	Skaði	A giantess associated with winter and skiing. Uncomfortably married to Njord.
Skjalf	Skjálf	A name for Freyja, meaning "shaker."

Sleipnir		Odin's eight-legged horse and the fastest of all horses.
Svadilfari	Svaðilfari	A mason's horse that Loki seduces as a mare.
Syr	Sýr	A name for Freyja, meaning "sow" in connection to pigs as a sacred animal.
Thor	Þórr	The thunder-god and protector of Midgard, who wields the hammer Mjolnir.
Throng	Thröng	A name for Freyja, meaning "throng."
Thrungva		A name for Freyja, meaning "throng."
Thrym	Þrymr	The giant who stole Thor's hammer and requests Freyja's hand in marriage in exchange for it.
Tregul & Bygul		The names of Freyja's cats, as coined by writer Diana L. Paxton in the mid-1980s.
Valfreyja		A name for Freyja, meaning "lady of the slain."

PLACES

English	Old Norse	
Alfheim	Álfheimr	The home of the light elves. It was given to Frey when he lost his first tooth.
Asgard	Ásgarðr	The home of the Aesir.
Bifrost	Bifröst	The rainbow bridge that connects Asgard to Midgard.
Folkvang	Fólkvangr	One of Freyja's halls, where half of the fallen warriors go. The other half go to Valhalla.
Helheim		The hall of the dead, where those who die of old age and sickness go.
Jötunheim	Jötunheimr	The home of the giants.
Midgard	Miðgarðr	["Middle Earth"] The home of people. The material world.
Muspelheim	Múspellsheimr	A fiery primordial world. Fire-giants live here.
Niflheim	Niflheimr	A cold and misty primordial realm of frost and ice.
Noatun	Nóatún	Njord's hall.
Nordic Countries, the		Norway, Sweden, Denmark, Iceland, Greenland, Finland, Åland, and the Faroe Islands.
Scandinavia		The historical name for a linguistic and cultural region in, Northern Europe, mostly correlating with the Nordic countries but also parts of Germany. Those from the Nordic countries still tend to refer to themselves as Scandinavian.
Sessrumnir	Sessrúmnir	One of Freyja's halls. It's also characterized as a field and a ship.

English	Old Norse	
Valhalla	Valhöll	The hall of the slain. Odin's hall, where fallen warriors go.
Vanaheim	Vanaheimr	Home of the Vanir, from which Freyja originates.
Yggdrasil		The World Tree, which holds all realms.

THINGS, CONCEPTS, AND EVENTS

English	Old Norse	
Aesir	Æsir	The principal family of deities within the Norse pantheon.
Black elves	Svartálfar	Black elves, possibly a cognate with dwarves and dark elves. They are said to live underground and be blacker than pitch.
Brisingamen	Brísingamen	Freyja's beautiful necklace, which shines like amber and was forged by the dwarves.
Dark elves	Dökkálfar	Elves who live underground and contrast with the light elves. See also *Black elves*.
Disir	Dísir	Female spirits associated with fate.
Dwarves	Dvergr	Beings who live deep beneath the earth and are masters of craftwork.
Einherjar		The warriors of Valhalla.
Galdrastafir		Icelandic magical staves.
Giants	Jötnar	Beings who embody the wild, untamable landscapes and forces of the world.
Heathenry		A neo-pagan spiritual movement centered on the beliefs, customs, and practices of various pre-Christian northern European societies.
Horg	Hörgr	An outdoor ritual altar.
Kenning		A kind of word play, which uses descriptive turns of phrase in place of a word, found in Old Norse poetry.
Land spirit	Landvættir	A spirit whose "body" is a certain area of land or land feature.
Light elves	Ljósálfar	Elves who are said to live in the realm of Alfheim and to be fairer than the sun to look at.
Mjolnir	Mjölnir	Thor's hammer.
Nisse		Friendly house spirits.
Norns, the	Nornir	Women who shape the course of fate and destiny.
Norse Paganism		A neo-pagan spirituality modeled after the beliefs, customs, and practices of the Norse people.
Offering	Blót	The act of making offerings to deities, ancestors, or spirits.
Ragnarok	Ragnarök	["The destiny of the gods"] The collapse of the Aesir's society.

Seid	Seiðr	A kind of Norse magic.
Thurs	Þurs	Giants who represent forces of nature that are actively hostile toward human life.
Tomte		See *Nisse*.
Trolls		A general word for a being who is "other." Can also be used to describe magic.
Valkyries	Valkyrjur	Women who ride over the battlefields and carry fallen warriors to Odin's hall, Valhalla, after they die.
Vanir		Another family of deities within the Norse pantheon, who fought a war with the Aesir in bygone times.
Viking Age, the		[793–1066 CE] A period marked by extensive sailing, trading, and raiding by the Norse people.
Web of Wyrd		Wyrd is the Norse concept of fate or destiny. The Web of Wyrd can be thought of as the interweaving of circumstances that surround us and the relationships of cause and effect, action and outcomes.
Wight	Vættr	A general term for "being" or "spirit."
Witch/Seeress	Völva (singular) Völur (plural)	["Staff-bearer"] A witch, seeress, or wise woman.
Wyrd		The relationship between cause and effect that creates the circumstances around us.

TEXTS

Our knowledge of the old Norse legends derives from a few main written sources, listed in bold type below. If you'd like to read them for yourself, I've specified which of the primary sources each "lay" or poem comes from.

Alvíssmál [1]	All-Wise's Sayings
Baldrs draumar [1] [3]	Balder's Dreams
Codex Regius, the	A manuscript from which the *Poetic Edda* is derived. It was written around 1270 CE.
Egils saga	Egil's saga. A medieval Icelandic saga. It's oldest manuscript dates back to 1250 CE.
Flateyjarbók	Book of Flatey. A medieval Icelandic manuscript compiled by two Christian priests in the 14th century.
Germania	[98 CE] A biased ethnography of the Germanic peoples written by the Roman historian and politician, Publius Cornelius Tacitus.
Gesta Danorum	The History of the Danes, written by Saxo Grammaticus in 1208 CE.
Gesta hammaburgensis ecclesiae pontificum	Deeds of the Bishops of Hamburg. By German medieval chronicler Adam of Bremen.
Grímnismál [1]	Grimnir's Sayings

Gróttasöngr [1]	The Mill's Song
Gylfaginning [2]	The Tricking of Gylfi
Hálfs saga ok hálfsrekka	The Saga of Halfr and His Heroes. A legendary saga about Halfr, who was one of Norway's most famous and legendary sea-kings.
Hárbarðsljóð [1]	The Lay of Harbard
Háttatal [2]	Tally of Meters
Hávamál [1]	Sayings of the High One
Heimskringla	A collection of sagas about Swedish and Norwegian kings of disputed authorship, though some scholars attribute it to Snorri Sturluson.
Hymiskviða [1]	The Lay of Hymir
Hyndluljóð [1]	The Lay of Hyndla
Lokasenna [1]	Loki's Quarrel
Lokka Þáttur	Loki's Song. It is a Faroese ballad potentially dating back to the 14th century.
Njáls saga	Njal's saga. The longest and most highly developed of the sagas of the Icelanders.
Oddrúnargrátr [1]	Oddrun's lament. An Eddic poem, likely from the 11th century.
Poetic Edda, the	A compilation of anonymous Old Norse poetry, dating from before Scandinavia converted to Christianity.
Prose Edda, the	Also called the *Edda* or the *Elder Edda*. It was written by Snorri Sturluson around 1220 CE.
Rígsþula [1]	The Lay of Rig
Skáldskaparmál [2]	Poetic Diction, The Language of Poetry
Skírnismál [1]	The Lay of Skirnir
Sörla þáttr	A passage contained in *Flateyjarbók*.
Vafþrúðnismál [1]	The Lay of Vafthrudnir
Völundarkviða [1]	The Lay of Volund
Völuspá in skamma [1]	Short Prophecy of the Seeress
Völuspá [1]	The Prophecy of the Seeress
Ynglinga saga	A King's saga, written by Snorri Sturluson, about the royal Yngling dynasty, contained in the first section of *Heimskringla*.
Þrymskviða [1]	The Lay of Thrym

Key:
[1] - Found in the *Poetic Edda*
[2] - Found in the *Prose Edda*
[3] - Found in *Gesta Danorum*

INDEX

A
Aesir, the 15
Aesir-Vanir War 19, 60–1
álfablót ("sacrifice to the elves") 42
Alfheim 16–17
Alvar 20
Asgard 15, 16–17, 70–1
Ásmundar saga kappabana 42

B
Bellows, Henry Adams 17, 54
blót (offerings) 96–102

C
cats 40–1, 49
cave system, Dordogne 58
Celts, the 19
Christianity 10
clairsenses 113
Codex Regius, the 13
confirmation bias 117
cosmology 14–17
courage ritual 114–15

D
deity interview spread 113
dísablót ("sacrifice to the Disir") 42
disambiguation 116
discernment, tools of 116–18
Dísir 21, 42
divination 112
Dvergr (dwarves) 21

E
Egils saga 42, 87
Einherjar 20
entities, norse 20–1

F
folklore, purpose of 12–13
Forging of Brisingamen 66–7, 87
Frey 15, 19, 46, 48
Freyja
  appearance 30
  archaeological finds 82–3
  associations 33–6
    beauty 19, 33
    death 34
    falcons 36
    fertility 19, 33
    girlhood, womanhood, femininity 36
    love 33–4
    rocks, minerals, and metals 53
    seid and magic 34
    sunlight 70
    war 34
  and cats 40–1
  characteristics
    seeress/völva 32
    Vanir 32
    warrior 32
  communicating with 111–13
    methods of 112–13
  and the Disir 42–3
  early modern-day representations 89
  exchanging 62
  family tree 46–9
  and flowers 38–9
    columbine 39
    cowslip 38
    daisy 39
    hemp 39
    snowdrop 38

  and jewelry 52–3
  in medieval folklore 88
  in medieval times 84–8
    in other sagas 87
    in the *Poetic Edda* 85–6
    in the *Prose Edda* 86
  in movies and on TV 90
  in mythology and folklore 56–79
  names 26, 82
  notable possessions
    Brisingamen (necklace) 37, 66–9
    chariot pulled by cats 37
    cloak of feathers 37
  part of the Aesir 15
  personality 27–9
    courageous 29, 114–15
    creative 29
    cunning and clever 27
    good sense of humor 29
    patient 29
    protective 27–9
    strong and powerful 29
    tempestuous 29
    tenacious and resolute 27
    wise 27
  in pop culture 90
  special days 110
  before and during the Viking Age 82–3
  who is Freyja? 10–11, 24–55
  in the world 80–91
Freyja Escapes Marriage 62–5
Freyja Rides with Hyndla 76–9
Freyja's Life in Asgard 70–1
Friday 110
Frigg 50–1

G

Gersemi 46, 48
"god," defining 14–15
Gullveig 54–5, 103
Gylfaginning 13, 86

H

Hakon, King 13
Hálfs Saga 42, 87
Heimdall Returns Freyja's Necklace 69
Helheim 19
Hildisvini 49
Hnoss 46, 48
Horn, Jan Sigurd 12
hygge 58–9
Hyndla 76–9

I

Iceland 13

J

jewelry 37, 52–3, 66–9
Jötnar (giants) 21
Jötunheim 16–17, 19

L

Landvættir (land spirits) 20
Lay of Hyndla 76–9

M

mental illness 117
Midgard 16–17
Midsummer 110
Muspelheim 16–17, 19
mythology, purpose of 12–13

N

Nidavellir 16–17
Niflheim 16–17
Nine Realms 16–17
Nisse/tomte 20
Njáls saga 87
Njord 15, 19, 46–7
Njord's sister 46–7
Nordic countries 10
Nornir 20
noticing 117

O

oaths, breaking 65
Od 46, 48
Odin 46, 49
oral traditions 13, 59
Ottar 46, 49

P

Paxton, Diana L. 40
Poetic Edda, the 13, 17, 54, 76–9, 85–6
popular media 90
Prose Edda, the 13, 86

R

Ragnarok 79

S

sagas 13, 42, 87
sandbox, the 116
seid and practicing seid 103–9
    concept of fate and the soul in Norse paganism 104–5
    function of 104
    modern 105–6
    in Norse societies 103
    practicing through
        divination 109
        fibercrafts 109
        trance/meditation 109
    training the senses 107–8
    Völur and 103
Skadi 46–7
Skáldskaparmál 13, 86
"sock puppet," mental 117
Sörla þáttr 87
Spring Equinox 110
Sturluson, Snorri 13
Svartalfheim 16–17
synchronicities 112

T

Theft of Freyja's Necklace 68–9
Theft of Thor's Hammer 72–5
Thor 72–5
Thurs 21
trolls 20–1

V

Valkyrjur (valkyries) 20
Vanaheim 15, 16–17, 19
Vanir, the 15, 19
Veneration practice 92–102
    building an altar 95
    how to 94
    offerings 96–102
Völur 21, 103
Völsunga saga 42
Völuspá 54, 85–6, 103

W

Wachtel, Edward 58
Wagner, Richard, "Das Rheingold" 89
Wights 20

Y

Yggdrasil 16

AUTHOR'S ACKNOWLEDGMENTS

I'd like to thank my editor, Charlene Fernandes, for her support, patience, and grace during the writing of this book; as well as Elinor Ward for her excellent knowledge in Norse studies and for cross-checking manuscripts. I'd also like to thank Lily De Gatacre for facilitating this project to begin with, as well as Emma Harverson, Caroline West, Martina Calvio, Karin Skånberg, and Lorraine Dickey for bringing it to life. Lastly, I'd like to thank the Saxon Storyteller for all his fantastic illustrations, and also my clergy, A. Ravenscroft (M.Div), for her assistance with Freyja's ritual and for her wisdom and advice regarding this goddess.

Thank you for reading and I hope you've enjoyed!

ABOUT THE ILLUSTRATOR

Matt Greenway is the illustrator of the Norse Gods series. He is known for his ability to capture the character of artifacts and historical figures and goes by "THE SAXON STORYTELLER" on the internet. His interests in Anglo Saxon, Celtic, and Norse mythologies and history have inspired his work for many years. He shares his passion for drawing mythology on Instagram @thesaxonstoryteller and illustrates content for the Nordic Mythology Podcast.